Check

Barn

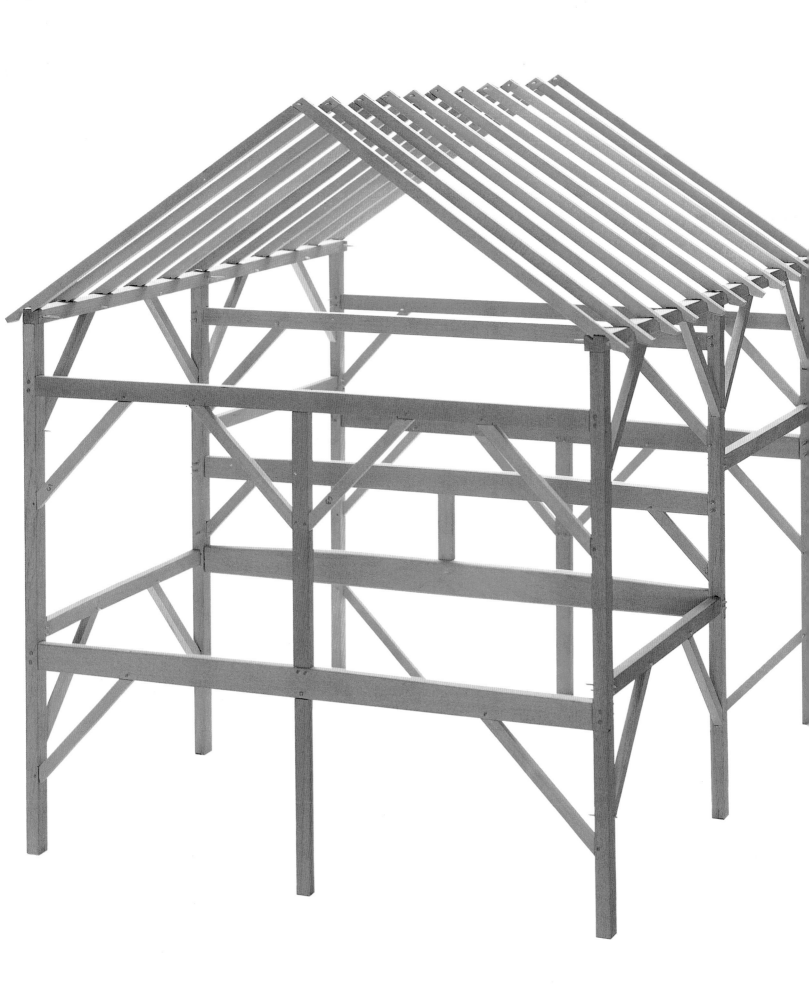

Barn

THE ART OF A WORKING BUILDING

BY ELRIC ENDERSBY, ALEXANDER GREENWOOD, AND DAVID LARKIN

Principal photography by Paul Rocheleau

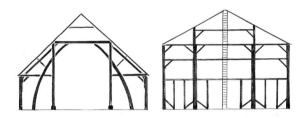

A David Larkin Book

Houghton Mifflin Company

Boston   New York   London

1992

Text copyright © 1992 by Elric Endersby and Alexander Greenwood
Compilation copyright © 1992 by David Larkin
All rights reserved.
For information about permission to reproduce
selections from this book, write to Permissions,
Houghton Mifflin Company, 215 Park Avenue South,
New York, New York 10003.

Library of Congress Cataloging-in-Publication Data
Endersby, Elric.
Barn : the art of a working building / Elric Endersby, Alexander
Greenwood, and David Larkin ; principal photography by Paul
Rocheleau.
p.   cm.
Includes bibliographical references.
ISBN 0-395-57372-6
1. Barns — United States.   I. Greenwood, Alexander.   II. Larkin,
David.   III. Title.
NA8230.E47   1992   92-16071
728′.922′0973 — dc20   CIP

Printed in Japan
DNP 10 9 8 7 6 5 4 3 2 1

CONTENTS

INTRODUCTION
9

ORIGINS
10

THE NEW WORLD BARN
59

RAISING
130

LIVING BARNS
177

GLOSSARY
250

BIBLIOGRAPHY AND ACKNOWLEDGMENTS
254

A barn in St. Michael, Minnesota

Introduction

A PROUD SILHOUETTE looming on the landscape, solitary or surrounded by ells, lean-tos, silos, or sheds, the barn commands attention, respect, even reverence. Drawn closer, the viewer's eye lingers on the rugged texture of weathered sheathing, the tilt of a weathercock pockmarked with birdshot, the repose of a listing silo, the forgotten portent of a faded hex sign. The barn's shadows, drawn diagonally from the varied massing of volumes, beckon the curious observer around each corner. Confronted with colossal doors, he or she is forced to find a gap for a stolen peek, then to slide aside a great door for a wider look and slip inside for a survey of the cavernous interior. Only then, after the viewer's eyes adjust to the darkness, does the structure come into clear view.

The lasting impressions gained from this experience are as varied as those who share it. The smell of horseflesh and fresh-cut hay; the moist, nuzzling nose of a cow in her stanchion; or the snorting breath of a foal, vaporous on a frigid morning. The swooping arc of a barn swallow, or the cool, all-knowing stare of an owl. The arched back of a stretching barn cat, or the cackling of a nesting hen. The discovery in a dark corner of a spiderweb or a vintage tractor. The easy, purposeful order of ropes or harnesses hung on pegs. The receptive grasp to the well-worn handle of a leaning rake or spade. The slanting rays of the sun cast through a knothole, or the view framed by the great threshing-floor doors. Feathery fingers of snow blown under a batten door. Rain on the roof.

Real or half remembered, such images reflect the warmth with which barns are widely regarded. Yet a more practiced, if prejudiced, eye may see in these structures a body of endeavor whose roots reach deep into the saga of western civilization. Here, unaltered in ancient European examples or synthesized, amended, and enlarged in America, is an irrefutable testimony to the integrity and economy with which builders shaped native materials into monumental structures.

Origins

NEARLY A MILLENNIUM has passed since the oldest barns still in existence were built in medieval Europe. As with so many other aspects of life in that era, the pervasive influence of the church affected their form. The vast landholdings of the monastic orders produced bountiful harvests that had to be protected. Tithes to the church, paid in grain, created the need for capacious warehouses. Like the cloisters and cathedrals built by the same hands, these huge buildings were largely laid up in stone and strengthened by an internal timber structure that divided the interior into a rhythm of bents and bays. Projecting porches marked the position of giant doorways, aligned to channel breezes through the barn for the winnowing of wheat.

Barns served the needs not just of the religious orders but of the gentry and the emerging yeomanry as well. Modestly proportioned, barns on manors and farms assumed different forms according to the climate and available building materials. In England, for instance, relatively warm winters meant that it was not necessary to stable most livestock, and barns were reserved for grain storage. Even after more studied husbandry developed, the structures that emerged were segregated by function both from the farmer's dwelling and from one another. The resulting barnyard might eventually include a stable, a cowhouse, a piggery, a sheepcote, a dovecote, and a coop for fowl. In addition, the wagon house, hop house, springhouse, smokehouse, granary, and buttery each performed a single function, leaving the central barn for the processing and storing of grain.

In northern continental Europe, harsh winters dictated the shelter of livestock for months at a time, and most animals were housed together under one roof. Stalls and stables were arranged around a central threshing floor, with insulating lofts above, from which hay could be easily pitched into the mangers. In the Low Countries in particular, keeping animals in these ubiquitous structures assured the accumulation of many months' worth of manure, which was used in the spring to enrich the land. Animals were not sheltered alone under these wide-roofed buildings; farmers and their families lived in them too. At first a pit in the center floor served as the hearth, and haymows insulated both humans and beasts. Though a few of these early barns survive, the most telling views of day-to-day farm life were left to us by limners and illustrators, who included the familiar barns of their day in genre paintings and depictions of the Nativity.

The materials from which barns were constructed depended on what was close at hand. Where frost heaves meant that farmers had to harrow stone from the fields every year, masonry construction made sense. In regions where clay was abundant, brick became the choice material. Elsewhere, the felling of timber to create arable fields prompted the construction of timber frames. Selected trees were toppled and then cured for a year or two, after which they were hewn into squared beams. These were made with projecting tongues, or tenons, and mortises, the notches that receive the tenons. Pegged together, they formed remarkably sturdy frames. Because these assemblies concentrated the weight of the building and its contents on widely spaced posts, the interior was largely unencumbered. Even masonry barns incorporated internal armatures of wood. The same building technology was employed in houses, churches, guildhalls, and market halls, but nowhere was the structure so fully realized as in the barns.

Although this tradition led to marvelously imaginative feats of engineering on a massive scale, its epoch in Europe was relatively short-lived. Except in the remotest regions, perhaps because of its very popularity, timber framing was doomed by the rapid depletion of the forests. In England, for example, after the threat posed by the Spanish Armada in 1588, all timbers longer than sixteen feet were reserved for the masts and spars of the Royal Navy. So it was that the timber-framing tradition might have degenerated into meaningless mannerism, if not for the colonization of North America beginning in the early seventeenth century.

By tradition, from medieval to modern times, the various needs of the farm have been satisfied by a variety of specific structures, such as cotes, coops, smokehouses, springhouses, stables, piggeries, wagon houses, and barns. Of these, the barn has always dominated the farmstead both in scale and in function.

At Weald and Downland, a museum of historic vernacular buildings from southern England, is a barn originally built at Lee-on-Solent. Its size, typical among local yeomen's farms, reflects the abundance of the annual harvests it once sheltered. Although it dates from the late sixteenth or early seventeenth century, the broad roof and projecting porch entry that define its profile were common features as early as the Middle Ages.

The Lee-on-Solent barn incorporates an oak frame, reed thatch, and oak weatherboard siding, all probably produced on or near the farm it served. The surrounding structures employ other materials — brick, tile, flint, and chalk — which were indigenous to their original locations.

Cressing Temple, in Essex, is the site of two remarkable early barns, each employed to store a specific crop. Both were built by the Knights Templars, a military order formed to protect pilgrims traveling to the Holy Land. Since the farm comprised seven hundred acres, considerable space was required for storing the harvest. The Barley Barn, with whitewashed walls, is the earlier structure, dating to about 1200. The Wheat Barn is thought to have been built around 1255. Both measure nearly 150 feet in length and are shielded by long tiled hip roofs with gablets, or small gables, at the ridge. Wagons loaded with crops passed through covered entrances known as wagon porches. When the farm at Cressing was acquired by the Essex County Council in 1987, both barns had been in continuous agricultural use for more than seven hundred years.

In *Far from the Madding Crowd,* Thomas Hardy describes a similar barn, "which on ground-plan resembled a church with transepts. It not only emulated the form of the neighboring church of the parish, but vied with it in antiquity. . . . One could say about this barn, what could hardly be said of either the church or the castle, akin to it in age and style, that the purpose which had dictated its original erection was the same to which it was still applied. Unlike and superior to either of those two typical remnants of medievalism, the old barn embodied practices which had suffered no mutilation at the hands of time."

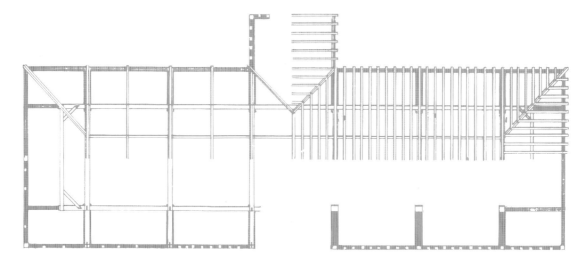

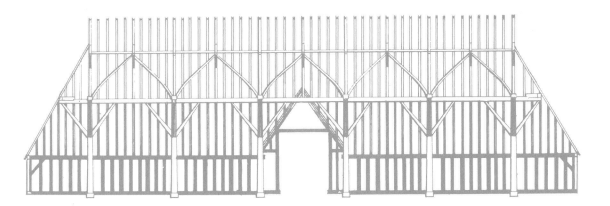

15

The enormous barns built to store the harvests of monasteries are known as grange barns. The oldest timber-frame barn in Britain is the grange barn at Coggeshall, Essex, estimated to have been built around 1140. Coggeshall Abbey was founded by King Stephen and absorbed in 1147 by the powerful and austere Cistercian order of the Benedictines.

In part because of a major rebuilding in the fourteenth century, the grange barn at Coggeshall survived more than eight hundred years of service as a working barn before twenty years of neglect in the 1960s and '70s left it in a state of partial collapse. An extensive and expensive restoration rescued this important building, which has now passed into the hands of the National Trust.

The interior of Coggeshall demonstrates perhaps the most dramatic of the English barn forms, the aisled hall. A soaring central nave flanked by lower side aisles creates a space much like that of a cathedral. Often aisles are included at the ends as well as at the sides. The tremendous weight of the roof is carried primarily by large interior columns known as arcade posts, with the balance resting on the perimeter. Small aisled barns have three bays, which are the spaces created by four parallel bents, or walls of framing. The grange barn at Coggeshall has six bays, with two wagon porches to provide access.

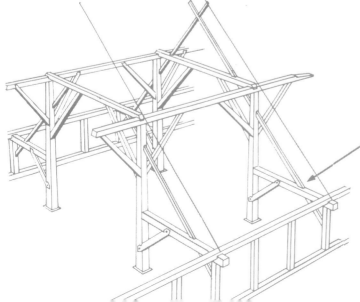

In light of the early date of construction for the grange barn at Coggeshall, the timber joints are of particular interest. For example, the open lap joint that ties a diagonal brace to a corner post is notched to resist withdrawal. This brace is considered a passing brace because it runs beyond the horizontal timber and continues on to the arcade post. Both the brace and the timber it passes are notched to form a lap joint. A hardwood peg, or trunnel (treenail), secures the connection.

Leigh Court barn was built for the monks at Penshore Abbey in Worcester early in the four-teenth century. It is remarkable principally as an example of cruck construction, the earliest and most organic form of assembly employed in English timber framing. Medieval builders sought out trees with an elongated curve, or cruck, from which timbers were cut, often halved, and then hewn into paired blades. When joined at the apex and stiffened with connect-ing collar ties and braces, these formed giant A-shaped trusses capable of transferring the weight of a vast roof directly to a padstone or a foundation wall. The earliest cruck frames were actually sunk into the ground.

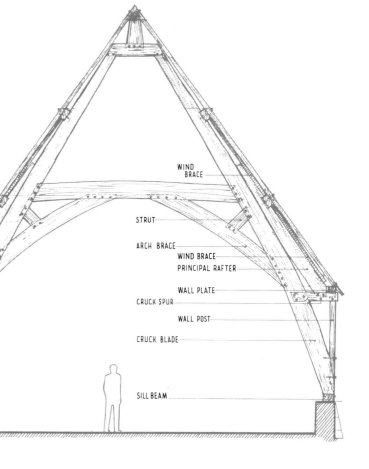

WIND BRACE

STRUT

ARCH BRACE

WIND BRACE

PRINCIPAL RAFTER

WALL PLATE

CRUCK SPUR

WALL POST

CRUCK BLADE

SILL BEAM

18

Once widespread in the Midlands, cruck frames were generally relatively modest in size. But Leigh Court is enormous, measuring 35 by 140 feet and requiring nine internal trusses, or bents. To build this barn, the barnwrights had to find eighteen trees of similar form from which to make individual blades fully thirty-six feet long. The parallel trusses, which are spaced about fourteen feet apart, are joined together by braced horizontal purlins and plates, which in turn support the rafters and thus the roof. The low walls, which carry virtually none of the roof's weight, were originally made of wattle — studs and slender staves through which oak withes were woven. Smaller crucks form the clipped gable walls and the two entry porches. Although larger cruck barns existed, they have gradually fallen back to the earth from which they sprang, and today Leigh Court is considered England's largest and most significant cruck structure.

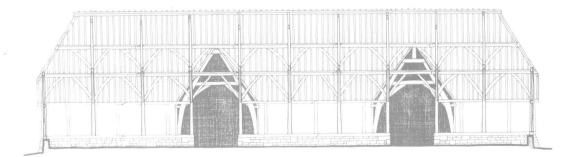

Not all cruck frames were as mighty as the one at Leigh Court. The barn at Cholstery Court Farm near Leominster, measuring only twenty-two by forty-four feet, is a well-preserved and well-restored example of the three-bay form common to small private farms. One of forty known cruck structures in Herefordshire, it has not been accurately dated, though a comparison with similar local examples indicates that it was built in the sixteenth century, near the end of the cruck tradition. Standing in the wake of farm modernization as a superfluous, deteriorating structure, it was disassembled in 1972, studied, repaired, and re-erected at nearby Avoncourt Museum.

During reconstruction, workers determined that the great cruck blades are of English black poplar, though the other timbers in the frame are oak. The rather poor quality of some of the cruck blades suggests that suitable timbers were already in short supply by the time of construction. A single surviving extended purlin provided evidence for the wide overhang of the restored barn; the thatched roof was based solely on local precedent. Stave holes and grooves indicated the original use of split oak panels for the low outer walls.

At an early date Herefordshire gained renown for growing cereal crops — wheat, barley, oats, and rye, known collectively in Britain as corn. In 1597 it was said in Parliament that while Shropshire might well become a "dayre" (dairy) house to the whole realm, Herefordshire and the adjoining counties were "the Barnes for the Corne." At harvesttime on farms like Cholstery Court, a portion of the crop was brought into the barn and placed at one end while the remainder was ricked in the yard. Then during the winter the harvested corn was hand-threshed and winnowed to separate grain from chaff.

This process defined the form of the English barn. In most cases, as at Cholstery Court, barns were arranged in three bays, of which the central one was left unobstructed as a threshing floor. This was shown on the outside by huge wagon doors nearly centered on both sidewalls, or broadsides, and inside by a smooth floor of stone flags or thick wooden planks. Farmhands could spread sheaves of grain on this floor and beat them with flails in a "whiplike rhythmical motion." This operation required room, and the threshing bay was therefore at least twice as high as the side bays, which often contained lofts.

Threshing also required dexterity and skill, as George Messenger, an elderly man schooled in the practice as a youth, recalled:

"When I fust used the flail I hit my self such a clout at the back o' the hid! It wholly hurt; the wood was some har! But the ol' boy along o' me said, 'Niver you mind, you'll git one or two of those afore you git the swing on it!' And I did, and I used to trash the corn I growed on my common yard for many years arter that."

After threshing, the big doors at both ends of the floor were thrown open and the grain was collected in broad, shallow winnow baskets and tossed in the air, so the draft caught the chaff and carried it from the barn as the grain fell to the floor. Encompassing the central operation of farm production, barns thus became something more than storage granges.

The Monks Barn at Harlow, Essex, is a tithe barn built at the beginning of the fifteenth century. Tithe barns were constructed on ecclesiastical estates to store tithes, the one-tenth share of income that rich and poor alike were required to pay to the church. These dues were commonly settled with corn, and the enormous structures built to house this bounty were used much like warehouses. Over time the phrase "tithe barn" was sometimes casually appropriated to describe grange barns, built for a monastery's own crops, or for the vast barns of the emerging secular estates.

The handsome oak frame of the Monks Barn is notable for the long curved passing braces that rise from the sill beams, pass the aisle posts, and finally join the tie beams. These graceful braces are thought to have been cut from trees grown especially for this purpose.

Despite having been blackened by fire, the
timbers of the Monks Barn remain structurally sound. Fortunately, the barn has been
thoroughly restored and now functions
as an exhibit hall and work area for the
Nettleswellbury Sculpture and Arts Center.

"The greatest piece of architecture in England" was the superlative lavished on the monumental barn at Great Coxwell, Berkshire, by William Morris, the nineteenth-century designer, who found it "unapproachable in its dignity, as beautiful as a cathedral yet with no ostentation of the builders' art." Like the cathedrals whose dimensions it approaches, the Abbey Grange at Great Coxwell is a stone structure. Like Coggeshall, it was undertaken by the Cistercian order, for whom the building of such warehouses was a high priority. Constructed in the mid-thirteenth century, it remained in agricultural use until 1966, when it passed to the National Trust, which has since undertaken an extensive study and restoration.

Measuring 43 by 152 feet, the barn soars to a height of 48 feet. Massive walls of Cotswold stone are reinforced by buttresses and punctuated by rows of ventilation holes and vertical slits, or loopholes. A transeptal porch divides each of its broadsides. Until entries were introduced at the gable ends of the barn in the eighteenth century, these porches were the only wagon openings.

English barns are almost universally entered from the sidewalls. Annual harvests could be unloaded only in the center bay, along the axis running from portal to portal — an inconvenience incumbent in a structure as long as Great Coxwell.

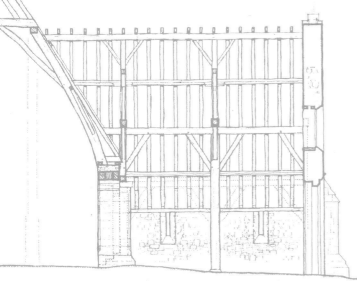

The entry porches at Great Coxwell, although different in dimension and design, exhibit many of the dominant characteristics of the barn itself. Dressed stone buttresses are placed to resist the greatest thrust. Surprisingly, the arched portals are segmental rather than gothic in form. Little is known of the original doors, except that they were hinged to open inward.

Above the portals, as elsewhere, holes that serve to ventilate the barn were originally employed to secure the short timbers, or putlogs, of the mason's wooden scaffolding to the rising structure. Capping stones protect the walls and, like the gables of the barn, once supported finials whose size and character have withered away into pure conjecture. The vast roof is made up of countless slabs of random Cotswold stone.

Given Great Coxwell's immense and impressive masonry shell, a similarly ecclesiastical interior of stone piers and gothic arches might be expected, and indeed the capacious space is divided into a twenty-one-foot-wide nave and two eight-and-a-half-foot side aisles. But the weight of the stone roof is borne by an ingeniously integral wooden skeleton featuring two rows of arcade posts, each bearing three pairs of acutely angled braces. The tensile strength of wood in this case replaces the bulk of stone.

Great Coxwell has "an interior timber frame with few equals in the medieval tradition," according to the architectural historian Walter Horn. "In no other structure of this kind are the basic structural capabilities of wood so forcibly and convincingly expressed: its ability to carry huge compressive loads on slender and remarkably high uprights, and its incredible tensile strength, enabling it to bridge intervals of extraordinary width and depth."

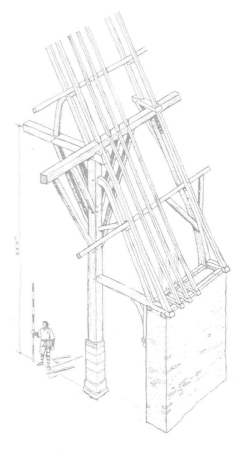

Arranged into six principal bents, posts twenty-two feet high rest on seven-foot stone piers. The posts and their supporting bases are separated by oak timbers laid sideways to prevent the transfer of moisture. The tie beams and primary purlins are fully thirty feet above the floor. To maintain the twenty-foot span between these principal bents, which creates a largely unobstructed floor, seven intermediate trusses made of giant cruck timbers rise from the buttressed outside walls to support the main purlin. In this way Great Coxwell juxtaposes alternating bents of the aisled-hall and cruck traditions in a building so well engineered that it remains structurally true after more than seven hundred years.

In France the local tradition of the aisled hall belongs not only to manorial barns but also to churches and market halls. An example exists in the Egreville market hall, which dates to the late sixteenth century.

The vertical timbers that rise from the center of the tie beams to support the ridge piece at the apex of the roof are known as king posts. These work in combination with the principal rafters and the tie beams, which connect each pair of opposing arcade posts, to form a king post truss. A variant form, the upper king post truss, employs a shorter king post bearing on a timber called a collar tie, which stretches horizontally between paired rafters; this provides better access to storage lofts. Nonetheless, the king post truss, which has been known since at least Roman times, is certainly the most common form of truss in French timber framing and is still used today.

The frame of the Arpajon market hall is strikingly similar to the one in Egreville. Scientific analysis of the growth rings of timbers suggests a construction date of 1480.

An elaborate aisled-hall timber frame was customary in important buildings such as market halls and the great barns of monasteries and manors. Needless to say, the barns of the average farmer were far more modest.

Throughout Europe it was an age-old practice to house people and animals under one roof, in a building loosely known as a long house or *une maison rudimentaire.* This dual-purpose dwelling took various forms in different ages and regions — some very crude, others quite sophisticated. The chimney placement reveals which end of this French barn house was reserved for humans.

Wood was the material of choice for farm buildings until it became scarce. Vernacular barns, though numerous, were small and often of simple cruck construction, which is found throughout northern and western France.

More prestigious and expensive framing, how-ever, employed close studding, in which many vertical timbers, or studs, were used. Common enough in urban architecture, this framing was too expensive for all but the most prosperous farmers. Perhaps to avoid breaking the rhythm of the studs, the frame of this barn in northern France is stiffened by saltire (X-shaped) braces, which are tenoned into the plates and girts and half-lapped where they pass. Brickwork, or nogging, fills the spaces between the studs.

A lane leads not only to a working farmstead at Nievwer Ter Aa in northern Holland but also to another cradle of barn tradition. Although these barns are nineteenth-century examples, they vary little from those built centuries earlier in the rich farmlands of the Netherlands. The barn to the left belongs to the nave-and-aisle form encountered in Britain but is differentiated by the entry on the gable end. The overhanging thatched hood served as a tie-up, or cow stable,

and included a hatch through which farmhands could pitch hay into the mow from wagons outside. The enfolding brick wall and external buttresses are atypical. The curious structure in the background is a hay barrack, an adjustable roof supported on poles to protect surplus hay. Shiploads of émigrés from the Low Countries who set out for the New World in the seventeenth and eighteenth centuries carried a familiarity with these building traditions.

overleaf

A large divided wagon door to the left opens inward from the gable end to reveal the typical interior of a Dutch barn. Based on the nave-and-aisle or basilica plan, Dutch barns are defined by substantial arcade posts that bear anchor beams big enough to span a wide threshing floor while supporting a roomy hayloft. Sheltered under a broad, steep roof extending to within a few feet of the ground, these barns are usually wider than they are long. The side aisles, reserved for live-stock, were often dug out below the level of the central threshing floor. Early examples usually included the residence, or house place, under the same roof. The door at the far end of the thresh-ing area leads to the farm kitchen.

A barn house built in Drenthe around 1700 exemplifies the most basic form of the ubiquitous long house, characterized by the absence of a wall between the areas inhabited by people and animals. Despite the primitive use of communal space, this type, known locally as *los hoes,* sur-vived into the twentieth century. One end was composed of the farm kitchen and its hearth, around which the family gathered to eat and sleep. At the other end was the squarish barn, with a central nave for threshing and low aisles for animal stalls. The entire structure was envel-oped in a thick thatched roof and walls of woven saplings packed in mud, known as wattle and daub. Together they provided remarkable insula-tion. Further, the body heat of the animals in their stalls immediately below the haymow aug-mented the warmth of the fire.

These stalls were dug out two feet or more below the threshing floor; then the farmer simply continued to spread layers of chopped straw and turf on the dung until the animals stood at the same level as the floor of the nave. When spring came, he would muck out the manure and spread it on the fields. Manure, in fact, was so valuable that it was a principal reason for keeping cows and sheep.

The constant presence of the fire at one end of the building helped dry and preserve the harvest in the lofts at the other. Another advantage, according to a nineteenth-century observer, was that "the woman of the house could sit at her spinning wheel keeping an eye not only on the fire, the food in the pot and the baby in the cradle, but also on all the livestock as well as the rest of the family at work in the barn, and could issue her orders without stirring from her chair."

Records for this diminutive *los hoes* at Harreveld, Gelderland, near Germany, can be traced to 1771. Although the low sidewalls are now laid up in brick, they were once like the surviving gable façade — timber framed and filled with wattle and daub. In accordance with local custom, the walls are blue-washed inside and out, perhaps as a means of warding off flies. The triangular opening in the thatch once vented smoke, in place of a chimney. The well sweep in the kitchen yard was a common device for raising water.

When this barn was built, small farms were primarily engaged in cultivating crops. However, by the mid-nineteenth century, animal husbandry had come to dominate farming in the region, and additional stalls and a piggery were added to the opposite end of the barn. Throughout history, as agricultural practices evolved, so did barns, in order to accommodate the changes.

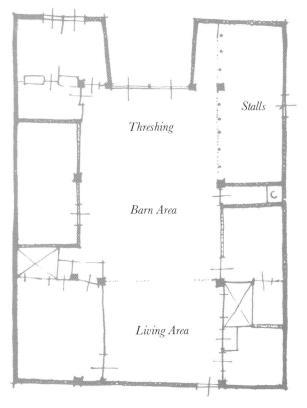

Stalls

Threshing

Barn Area

Living Area

Connected farmlands such as this one from
Midlum in Friesland were common in the region
northeast of Harlingen known as Bouwhoek, an
area endowed with rich marine clay soils well
suited to productive farming. Rebuilt in 1778 to
plans that still exist, the Midlum barn house
belongs to a type known locally as head, neck,
and body. The head consists of a compact house
containing a parlor and sleeping quarters and is
very like contemporary nonagricultural town-
houses. The neck and the shoulder end of the
barn behind it are given over to the domestic
industry of the kitchen, churning room, and milk
cellar. Although the body of the barn is built on
the basilica plan, the large doors open not into
the central nave but into a separate passage in
one side aisle. Stalls occupy the opposite aisle.
The threshing floor at the far end of the nave is
independent of the wagon passage. Since good
clay is plentiful in the area, both house and barn
are built of brick. The roof of the house is of clay
tile, but the barn employs both tile and thatch,
another local tradition, designed and laid down
in geometric patterns.

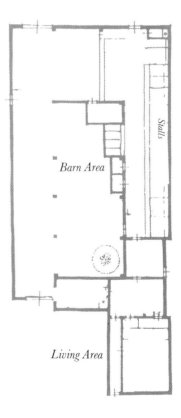

Stalls

Barn Area

Living Area

overleaf

The anchor beams, braces, and rafters of yet
another small Dutch barn display a pleasing
irregularity. In Holland such crooked members
are not related to the English cruck tradition,
wherein builders actively sought curved timbers
as an integral part of the framing. Rather,
they are the unavoidable result of a scarcity of
long, straight beams. Without a domestic supply
of suitable building materials, the Dutch went
so far as to float logs from Scandinavia for
their structures.

The whitewashed wall marks the insertion of a
separate living area, or house place. Despite a
haymow above this space, the primitive quality
of the dwelling is offset by the connecting door,
richly grain-painted to resemble fine wood. In
fact, much of the appeal of house barns such
as this lies in the way fine detail is juxtaposed
with simple and purely functional parts of
the building.

In common with most working barns, this
example near Nieuwegein, Utrecht, includes a
number of modifications made to its frame by
generations of farmers. The relative importance
of the anchor bent assembly is expressed by the
generous dimensions of the post, brace, and
anchor beam. These are square and hewn, in
contrast to the long undressed poles that serve as
purlins and rafters. The jerkinhead roof, which
extends well beyond the outside bent of the barn,
acts as a protective hood and provides the opportunity for an entirely open gable end, with no
wall or doors.

"A framework consisting of four heavy corner posts and a thatched straw roofing, which could be raised or lowered upon these corner posts, was called by the farmers a *barrack*. One or more of these barracks was in every farmyard for the straw and hay and served to relieve the over-crowded barns in seasons of a bountiful harvest." So wrote Gertrude Lefferts Vanderbilt in 1882 of the typical early farms of the Dutch New World.

The origin of the barrack is unknown. Prevalent throughout the north German plain from the Rhine delta to the Ukraine, this straightforward farm structure is most often found in the northern Netherlands, where it is still commonly used. Barracks also appear in Britain, where, confusingly, they are referred to as Dutch barns. The posts, which may be up to fifty feet high, are buried about five feet in the earth. Regularly spaced holes bored in these poles receive metal spikes, on which the movable roof is carried.

The simplicity of the structure made it ideal during the initial Dutch settlement of the New World, but exposure of the poles to the weather condemned most barracks to rapid deterioration. American examples were generally about eighteen feet square, with hip or close-gabled roofs. Dutch barracks are often borne on five or six posts. The umbrella-like single-stem variation from central Holland is rare.

overleaf

This surprisingly finely furnished farm kitchen is the only domestic feature in an otherwise utilitarian barn. The building was constructed around 1800 in Staphorst, Overijssel, where traditional practices lingered longer than in other regions of the Netherlands. Local elements include a jambless fireplace, cupboard beds, and the extensive use of tile on the floor and walls. The decorative painted furniture is a rural reflection of the Biedermeier style. Farms in the vicinity were rarely prosperous, and most of the men had to find seasonal work elsewhere, often in Germany. As a result, much, if not all, of the daily farmwork fell to the women.

Relocated near Hamburg are several northern German barn houses, of which this one, from Volksdorf, is a good example. Under a broad, encompassing thatched roof are both the barn, built on the basilica plan, and a two-story house. The slender timbers of the frame, left exposed to the weather, suggest a somewhat later date of construction than the Dutch and Danish examples. The brick housefront seems undistinguished compared with the lively herringbone pattern on the barn façade. This may reflect the relative importance of the barn and the family living quarters on farms of the period.

As demonstrated by English examples, the principal function of early barns was to provide roofed protection for annual harvested crops. Outside walls were generally low except where elevated porch entries projected to accommodate the wagon doors. But in this barn in Schleswig-Holstein, the notion has obviously been carried to an extreme.

The opening in the gable is a martin hole, providing free access for the graceful birds that are highly regarded as hunters of flying insects. The gap in the center of the roof forms an oculus, which lends light to the otherwise forbiddingly dark interior; it is placed over the threshing floor, where moisture cannot harm the mows. The wheel-like device at the far end is intended to attract storks for nesting.

The barn required a surrounding fence to prevent livestock from eating the roof — a practice that may have hastened the decline of this particular barn form!

Through the use of interlaced horizontal and vertical timbers, known as square panel framing, German barn builders were able to decrease the relative dimensions of the principal posts and tie beams. In the Untiedt barn, a secondary angled timber at the base of the rafters introduces the kick to the roof.

Built in 1791 near Wilmsdorf in northwestern Germany, this barn exhibits a jerkinhead roof reminiscent of earlier structures in England and elsewhere, but the placement of the wagon doors on the gable end betrays its northern European nave-and-aisle plan. Smaller doors at the sides provided access to animal stalls. Again martin holes are a prominent device. The complexity of the exposed frame and the playful patterns of the brick-and-stone infill clearly demonstrate the emergence of a decorative tradition, which gave the barn a new prominence on the farm.

This barn, built by Joachim Untiedt in 1797 near Barsbek in Germany, boasts a geometric harmony of brick and timber. Fanlights provide winter light to the threshing floor, and martin holes assume the form of the cross. A winnowing basket now leans against one of the inwardly hinged wagon doors, a reminder of the days when the barn was central to agricultural industry.

Wagon doors in Germany, like this great door at Pfarrhaus Grube, were treated with the respect usually reserved for the ceremonial portals of a church or public building. Often they were emblazoned with the name of the builder and descriptions of the circumstances attending construction. Protected by a pent or penthouse roof supported by crucked braces is a legend identifying 1569 as the year when Pastor Jeremias Striker zur Wohnung built this barn. The stave-like battens in the door form an intriguing pattern, which, like the crucked braces top and bottom, appears to be entirely decorative.

This farmstead from Ostenfeld, southern Schleswig, proclaims the name Hans Pettersen and the date 1685 over the wagon doors; however, it may well have been built at least a century earlier. The façade shows exposed framing of relatively hefty timbers, stained an unexpected blue and filled in with yellow brick made of local clay. The structure exemplifies the most primitive form of barn house in northern Europe. Built on the basilica plan, with central nave and lower side aisles, it does not separate areas that sheltered humans and animals. The nave served the family as a common room and also, in season, as a threshing floor. The fire, around which all the farm's occupants gathered for warmth, was built in a pit in the clay floor. Hay and straw in the mow above offered insulation. There was no chimney, even for the bake oven, and smoke simply escaped through the doors or out a small hole high in the thatched roof.

A passageway for wagons. At one end the area is open; at the other, a door within a door has been hung. When necessary, this area could serve as a haymow. The mow typically was supported by unattached poles cut from saplings, known as mow poles, which could be removed one by one so hay would tumble down as needed. Large bricks, locally called friarstones, make up the infill, which has been whitewashed.

Built at Eiderstedt in southwestern Schleswig in 1653, this farmstead typifies a form that first became popular from Holland northward around 1600, when increasing corn prices necessitated larger barns. This single structure encompasses all the central functions of the farm. The east end contains a gabled three-story house section. To the south, the threshing area is identified by its wagon doors. To the west are stables for horses and calves, and to the north cow stalls. These so-called outshots radiate from the central barn frame, formed by two enormous anchor bents supporting extended purlins. The thatched hip roof rises to a height at the ridge of forty-four feet. Such barn houses were generally built on artificially raised mounds surrounded by drainage dikes.

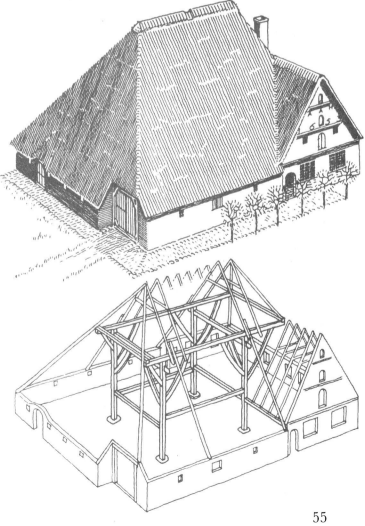

Log structures developed naturally in Scandinavia, where timber is plentiful. This connected barn and byre was built in 1744 at Engan, Os i Glåmdal, in Norway, then moved to the world's first open-air museum, at Oslo, in 1885. It is composed of two boxlike pens connected by a continuous sod-covered roof. The birch logs that surround this earthen covering are especially resistant to rot. The chimney marks the presence in one of the pens of a fireplace, a customary and understandable feature in the region. The passage between the pens, known as a *skjaele,* may be a forerunner of the so-called dogtrot barns of the New World.

The galleried form of barn construction exemplified by this log structure was native to northern Sweden in the sixteenth and seventeenth centuries. Even the lean-tos are built of logs. Despite the solidity and obvious weight of the building, the foundation consists merely of load-bearing padstones strategically positioned under critical sections of the log walls. These and the short penthouse roof over the wagon doors are features also found in early New World structures.

opposite

Dating to about 1800, this representative barn complex from Jorgedal in Bö, Norway, includes a stable and sheepcote constructed of squared and notched timbers. The lower story of the stable contains stalls and an area for fodder. The cantilevered upper story holds the haymow, which is reached through a hooded doorway at the top of a remarkably steep ramp.

The tradition of Swiss barn construction includes examples built of stone rubble, notched logs, and exposed heavy timber framing, or *fachwerk*. Though many of the earliest barns were attached to houses, separate structures were common as well. An area to the west of Lucerne known as Entlebuch is one of several regions where a feature called the forebay emerged.

Here, barns were built into the slopes of the hillsides, creating a ground floor in which to house livestock. The level above, used for threshing and storing hay, extended out over the downhill side. This projection, the forebay, was generally cantilevered, with additional support occasionally provided by either posts or braces. While no specific record of its intended purpose exists, this kind of barn offered several design advantages. The forebay sheltered the livestock from rain and high summer sun. More important, it deflected the heavy snows that slid from the roof, so they did not interfere with the operation of the stable doors below.

In this example from Entlebuch, a shallow, cantilevered forebay is supported by the projecting foundation logs, trimmed to resemble brackets. The double doors beneath the forebay lead to a wagon shed between two rows of stables.

The barn in Canton Schwyz, in central Switzerland, displays an elliptical gable soffit. A decorative feature common to Swiss houses and occasionally barns, this device also serves to protect the ends of the plates and purlins of the roof structure that extend beyond the gable wall.

The New World Barn

IN HINDSIGHT, it seems incredible that any but the most wretched or foolhardy would have undertaken the danger and hardship of being among the first European settlers of the New World. Confined for weeks in cramped quarters on an ocean that was overwhelming in both its monotony and its occasional ferocity, the colonists must have been exhilarated at making landfall, only to have that exhilaration swiftly tempered by the daunting prospect of mastering an untamed wilderness.

Armed with only a few tools and limited skills, they first had to provide shelter for themselves and the few domestic animals they had brought along. Establishing sustaining crops from their precious parcels of seed also took on a desperate importance. In America, as in Europe, where stone and clay lay in the path of cultivation, dwellings and outbuildings were made up of these materials. But nearly everywhere along the east coast of the new continent, the first sight beyond the shore-line was a seemingly endless forest. An impediment to the farmers, these stands of virgin trees promised sturdy structures of grand scale to the timber framers. Because of the density of the forests, trees were forced to grow straight for the light, their branches withering and leaving only small knots in the even grain. In New England, though hardwoods were numerous, pine and hemlock were the preferred species for barn frames. In Pennsylvania and New Jersey, the forests yielded enough white oak to frame most of the early barns; chestnut and tulip poplar were secondary choices. Because oak is such a strong wood, it is in this region that some of the most dramatic spans are found. Farther south, yellow pine augmented oak as a favored material.

Early timber-frame barn designs depended very much on the national tradi-tions of those who built them. English settlements took hold in the North and coastal South, Dutch in the areas spreading out from New Amsterdam (New York), and Swiss-German in Pennsylvania, as well as to the south and west along the Appalachian Mountains.

Little remained static in America. Some traditional building materials were almost immediately forsaken. Thatched roofs were not common, although straw was used on early Pennsylvania barns; roof tiles, so prevalent in the Old World, were not produced in significant quantities; and slate became popular only later, in the nineteenth century. Instead, white cedar, which flourished in coastal bogs and swamplands, could easily be split into durable roofing shingles. While wattle and daub and brick were widely used to fill in between the studding of houses, they were almost never used in barns. Many barns were sheathed in shingles, or, following the precedent of Dutch or Kentish clapboard, in wide riven or pit-sawed weatherboards. Vertical barn siding was rare until rudimentary sawmills were commonplace. Indeed, wood was so plentiful that in areas where little iron was available, wood was fashioned into hinges and other hardware — even nails for siding.

Farming practices inspired further alterations. For example, English settlers immediately discovered that New England winters were far too severe for their precious livestock to survive unprotected. Consequently, they set aside an aisle beside the threshing floor for the seasonal shelter of their animals.

Foremost among the factors contributing to the evolution of vernacular barn framing was the interchange between neighboring colonists from diverse national backgrounds. Since no farmer or framer could raise a structure as substantial as a barn by himself, the entire community was called upon to participate. Where framing techniques from different traditions came into contact, the best characteristics of each system were gradually combined into wholly American hybrid forms. As settlement pressed west from the seaboard, some of these new forms were in turn modified and improved.

In the aftermath of the Civil War, the United States became a more unified nation, not only politically but culturally. As railroads crossed the country, regions that had already exhausted their supplies of virgin timber could easily import sawed softwoods from the vast forests of the West. Meanwhile, advances in printing permitted wide dissemination of pulp magazines on every subject, including agricultural innovation. Among the notions made universally popular by these publications were safety, sanitation, and air circulation. The resulting additions of louvers, ventilators, silos, sliding doors, manure carriers, hayfork tracks, lightning rods, and the like came to define the barns of the period. Lighter building forms, including balloon frames and arched-truss roofs, were also popularized by this means, and with them came the close of the timber-frame era. Only in the last generation has an appreciation of barns and the timber-frame tradition they embody stimulated a revival.

Whereas in England the barn functioned as a storehouse for grain and hay while livestock were frequently left unsheltered, the harsh New England winters forced farmers to house their animals. Consequently, livestock stalls were introduced to the barn, generally in a bay to one side of the threshing floor.

Any comparison of barn framing in the Old and the New World affirms the remarkable size and regularity of the fine timbers yielded by the abundant forests of America. By the eighteenth century, only curved and irregular timber was available in Europe, which had been largely deforested. The long straight timbers of North America allowed greater span and thus a somewhat simpler barn frame design than was common in Europe.

A comparison between the Cholstery Court barn in Herefordshire and an eighteenth-century barn from Braintree, Massachusetts, recently re-erected at Old Sturbridge Village, shows the same basic form: each has three bays with a central threshing floor. Although the methods of construction were nearly identical, the long, straight timbers available in New England simplified the job of framing. The jerkinhead roof, common in England, was not adopted in the New World; perhaps because lumber was so plentiful, the English colonists used board roofs and later wood shingles after early experiments with thatch. Similarly, the English custom of filling in exposed half-timbered walls with brick or with wattle and daub proved to be impractical where extremes of temperature caused destructive expansion and contraction of building frames. By the beginning of the seventeenth century, New England barns were typically covered with split oak clapboarding to make them weathertight. Later, as settlements developed, sawmills provided inexpensive wide pine planks, and by the mid-1800s most barns were framed to receive vertical board siding.

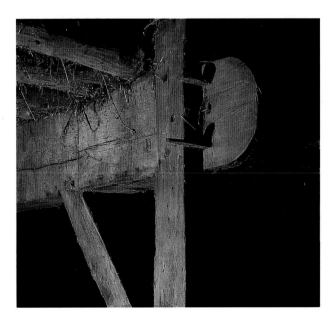

A Ferrisburg, Vermont, barn frame from the early nineteenth century has three bays established by four bents. This type is variously known as an English, Yankee, or Connecticut barn. Though this is the most common configuration, some examples have only two bays and others four or more. Very often bays were added to existing barns to meet growing needs. The posts of the bents are connected by horizontal timbers called girts, spaced about four feet apart in order to receive vertical pine siding.

A narrow English barn would typically have rafter pairs that were unsupported at midspan, but a wider frame such as this one, which measures thirty feet across, employs a purlin system to prevent rafters from shifting or collapsing. Here canted queen posts, otherwise known as inclined purlin struts, gracefully transfer the roof load from the purlins down to the tie beams. Nine additional sets of rafters complete the roof frame. Wide irregular pine boards nailed to the rafters form a base for a wood shingle roof.

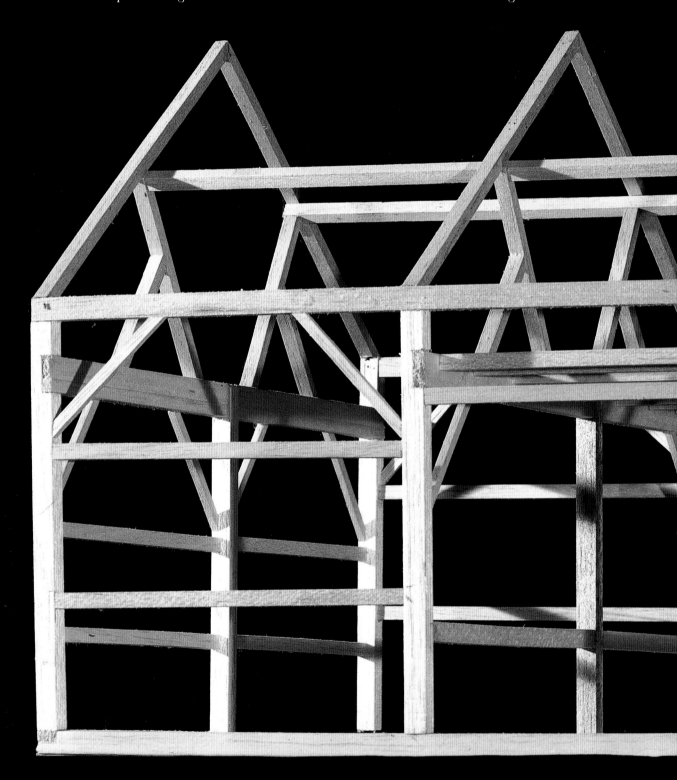

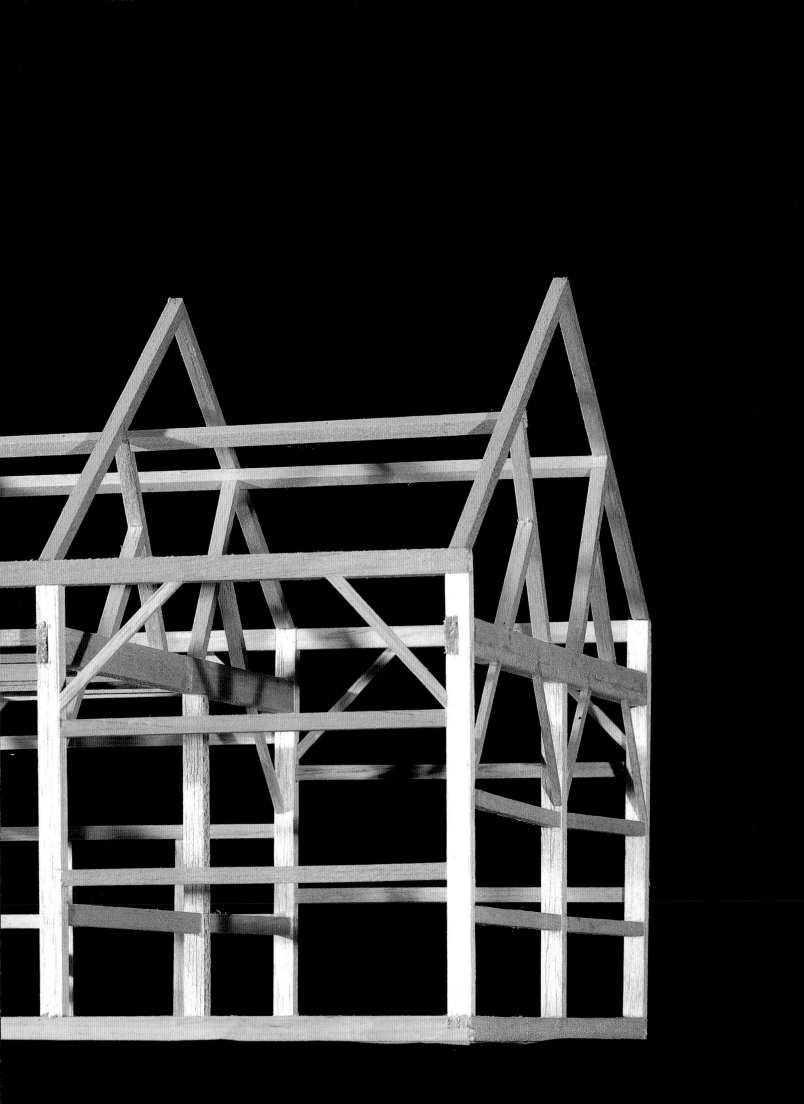

Some nineteenth-century Yankee barns incorporated a frame design that did not occur in England. The impressive swing beam is a timber that is large and strong enough to span the full width of the barn and support a hayloft without interim posts. This provided enough unobstructed indoor space for the ancient process known as flooring: the farmer would place bundles of hay in the middle of the barn and lead his horses or oxen round and round over them, in order to separate the grain from the chaff.

A sturdy mid-nineteenth-century barn built near Flemington, New Jersey, features a swing beam incorporated into a king post truss. In the years following the Civil War, steel rods were widely used along with timbers to form trusses for long spans.

In Dutch barns, in both the Old and the New World, the anchor beam is often the only member that prevents the building from spreading apart because of the outward thrust of the roof. A distinctive joint handles the tension at the juncture of the anchor beam and the arcade post. The Dutch reasoned that lengthening the tenon beyond the peg hole would help counter that tension by increasing the area of resistance. The protruding tenon, or tongue, that resulted might be gracefully rounded, squared, or tapered but was typically uniform within a particular barn.

Many English barns in America, particularly early ones, include a distinctive corner joint of medieval origin. The gunstock post flares near the top to provide bearing for both the plate and the tie beam. The end rafter is mortised into the tie beam instead of resting directly on the plate, as in most other framing systems. This beautiful but complicated arrangement attests the tenacity of building traditions.

The English barn type is not restricted to the early British colonies in New England and the coastal South. Many examples exist in the mid-Atlantic states and along the routes of settlement across the upper Midwest. These barns are most often built close to the ground on a low foundation wall, but some perch on foundations that are cut into the slope of a hill. This well-maintained New Jersey barn is clad on the gable wall with shingles, a siding material popular in coastal regions where cedar was plentiful. The original hinged doors have been replaced by sliding doors.

Although the English barn was the standard design in early New England, over the course of the nineteenth century there was a gradual shift to a gable-entry type known as the New England barn. Probably the most familiar barn form in the Northeast today, variations of the New England barn can be found throughout the nation. Often a long transom is set above the wagon doors, providing much-needed light for the interior.

Writing in 1748 of the peculiar structures he observed between New Brunswick and Trenton, New Jersey, Swedish traveler Peter Kalm essentially defined the form of what has come to be called the New World Dutch barn:

"The barns had a peculiar kind of construction in this locality, of which I shall give a concise description. The main building was very large, almost the size of a small church; the roof was high, covered with wooden shingles, sloping on both sides, but not steep. The walls which supported it were not much higher than a full grown man; but on the other hand the breadth of the building was all the greater. In the middle was the threshing floor and above it, or in the loft or garret, they put the unthreshed grain, the straw, or anything else, according to the season. On one side were stables for the horses, and on the other for the cows. The young stock had also their particular stables or stalls, and in both ends of the building were large doors, so that one could drive in with a cart and horses through one of them, and go out at the other. Here under one roof therefore were the threshing floor, the barn, the stables, the hayloft, the coach house, etc."

Distribution of this barn form reflected patterns of Dutch settlement, radiating from New Amsterdam (New York) to Long Island in the east, up the Hudson to the north, thence to the west along the Mohawk, and to the southwest across central New Jersey. Barns throughout this region were remarkably like one another, even though they differed in many aspects from the European precedent.

below

As demonstrated by an early example near Holmdel, New Jersey, New World Dutch barns are distinguished by a broad, steep, encompassing roof rising from low sidewalls. Long split shingles were used to sheath many Dutch barns in New Jersey and Long Island; otherwise, wide clapboards, or occasionally vertical siding, were employed. Centered under the gable are large wagon doors, often accompanied by a smaller door for human access. Frequently a shallow penthouse roof serves as protection for these openings. The wide doors at the corners lead to side aisles, where draft animals and dairy cows were housed.

Framed between the opposing wagon doors, the silhouette of an ox being yoked on the threshing floor is picturesque, if unexpected. New World Dutch barns, which followed the basilica plan, strictly consigned livestock to the flanking aisles, threshing and wagon storage to the nave. According to Kalm, the Dutch "preserved the custom of their country and generally kept their cattle in barns during the winter." Following European precedent, the earthen-floored stalls were often several feet below the level of the threshing floor. A giant haymow over the nave and smaller mows over the pens were supported by sapling mow poles, which could be pulled out one by one so the hay would tumble into the stalls. Cut into the wide weatherboards high above the wagon doors in a variety of patterns, martin holes were made big enough to encourage small birds such as martins and barn swallows to enter, but small enough to exclude unwelcome pigeons. In addition to providing passage for birds, these holes improved ventilation. Behind even the most decorative features of the New World Dutch barn were ingeniously practical decisions.

"The barns of the Dutch farmers were broad and capacious. The roof, like that on their houses, was very heavy, and sloped to within eight or ten feet of the ground. There were holes near the roof for the barn swallows that flitted in and out. . . . Through the chinks of broken shingles the rays of the sun fell across the darkness as if to winnow the dust through the long shafts of light, or, where the crevice was on the shady side, the daylight glittered through like stars, for there were no windows in these barns; there was light sufficient when the great double doors, large enough to admit a load of hay, were open."

— GERTRUDE LEFFERTS VANDERBILT, 1882

The cultural historian John Fitchen was the first to bring scholarly scrutiny to the New World Dutch barn. His lyrical description well suits this silhouetted barn from Guilderland, New York, which he documented years before its removal to Sleepy Hollow, New York, in 1982:

"New World Dutch barns are of noble proportions on the exterior: broad, capacious looking, spreading expansively to either side of the central wagon doors, above which the roof rises in complicated symmetry. These barns are big, but not overwhelmingly so. The simplicity of their shape is frankly utilitarian, but not impersonally or austerely so. Doors — even the Dutch door of the wagon entrances — are for human use, too: and both these and the martin holes above them combine usefulness and concern for good husbandry with an unselfconscious sense of good design. The shape of these barns is neither squat and sunken looking nor narrow and tall. Even when they are viewed from a distance there is a quality of integrity about them: an integrity of purpose, of materials and craftsmanship, of complete adaptation to the conditions of their being."

opposite

The wagon doors of the restored Guilderland barn at Sleepy Hollow open inward to the threshing floor in the European fashion. The wooden hinges and the pintles on which they pivot are copied from examples discovered in an early Dutch barn near Saratoga. Such pioneer features were soon supplanted by forged replacements as metal hardware became available.

The Schenk barn, a typical New World Dutch barn, was built in Dutch Neck, New Jersey, around 1780. Central to the scheme are the massively timbered anchor-bent assemblies. This barn, at thirty-five by forty-eight feet, includes four bents; larger examples might have as many as eight. The arcade posts measure about one foot square. The crowned anchor beams are ten by twenty inches at their center and thirty feet long, including the semicircular tongues. Outside posts are proportionately smaller, but like most New Jersey examples correspond directly to the number of arcade posts, to which they are tied by lateral girts. In the Hudson River country, however, outside walls were often framed with a row of posts about five feet apart.

As American agriculture prospered, harvests began to exceed the capacities of the barns built by an earlier generation. In considering the most effective way to expand, farmers in areas where cultures mingled often adapted their designs to incorporate the best features of another framing tradition. In New Jersey the Dutch and English lived side by side, no doubt laboring together to raise one another's barns. In Dutch Neck, New Jersey, a farmer of Dutch descent opted to double the volume of his haymow by raising the barn roof and turning it ninety degrees. The resulting gable profile was more English than Dutch.

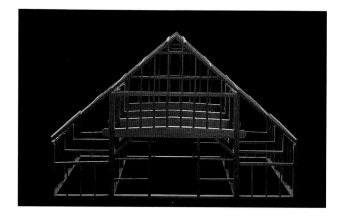

To effect this conversion, the roof was stripped and the rafters removed. A second set of posts was placed atop each sidewall so those walls were the same height as the arcade posts. The new forty-eight-foot-long plates and purlins, now running perpendicular to those they replaced, supported the shortened and reoriented rafters. Clearly this innovative scheme meant that the barn was laid bare, and therefore it must have been undertaken during the busy months of spring and summer, when neither harvests nor livestock needed shelter.

The shingled barn from Marlboro, New Jersey, has the same plan as the Schenk barn, not as a conversion but as a true New World Anglo-Dutch hybrid.

While New England and the Chesapeake Bay area were colonized primarily by the English, the settlers who established farms in southeastern Pennsylvania in the eighteenth century were largely of German and Swiss origin. Some of these immigrants were familiar with the forebay barns of central and eastern Switzerland. In the initial period of settlement, before the American Revolution, many different barn types were built in southeastern Pennsylvania. The practical advantages of the forebay, primarily the protection it afforded to the space below, must have been obvious, since this barn plan, in various versions, was widely adopted as the standard design by the nineteenth century.

above

This Swiss barn from Canton Schwyz is an example of the European prototype for the Pennsylvania, or Sweitzer, barn. The forebay is supported by an arcade, which repeats the shape of the gable soffit. Flower boxes embellish the foundation wall.

opposite

The syncopation of stable doors and windows in the stone foundation of this forebay barn in Lancaster County, Pennsylvania, is in pleasing contrast to the order and symmetry it otherwise expresses. Visible under the forebay are the long timbers serving as joists for the floor above. These rest on the foundation wall and in turn support the upper barn frame.

74

A seemingly random juxtaposition of rooflines and materials reflects the evolution of agriculture. Raised by a Chester County, Pennsylvania, farmer around 1800, the original barn with stone gable ends was built into the slope of a south-facing hill. Later, when cold storage allowed farmers to expand dairying beyond the immediate needs of their families, the long extension was added. Progressive ideas introduced by popular agricultural journals during the latter years of the nineteenth century inspired the construction of the silo. Like the families who built them, barns grew and changed from generation to generation.

The forebays of Chester County are noted for their extreme depth, a condition that strains the limits of a cantilevered frame. To provide additional support, the builders introduced ponderous stone pillars, based perhaps on English and Welsh precedent. The same device was used on this barn, not for the unsupported forebay but under the tie-up, where cows were sheltered while being fed directly from the hayloft above. The conical stone pillars were typically plastered smooth and whitewashed, both to discourage vermin and to protect the livestock from sharp stone edges. The block on top of the column strategically bears the load under the splayed scarf joint. Here again, beauty in barn details is born of practicality.

The Charles barn in Lancaster County follows the Pennsylvania German, or Sweitzer, tradition. In particular, it exemplifies the double-barn form adopted on larger farms, primarily west of the Susquehanna River. Constructed with five rather than four bents, it has an extra bay, which provided a second threshing floor. Historian Alfred Shoemaker has traced the term "double barn" through farm-sale notices back to 1782. The separate lean-to sheds in stone and frame on the upland side are later additions.

"Farmers in Pennsylvania have a commendable spirit for building good barns, which are mostly of stone. On the ground floor are stalls in which their horses and oxen are fed hay, cut-straw, and rye-meal; but not always their other beasts. Roots are seldom given to their live-stock, being too little thought of. The second floor with the roof, contains their sheaves of grain, which are thrashed on this floor. A part of their hay is also here stored. Loaded carts and wagons are driven in, on this second floor; with which the surface of the earth is there level; or else a bridge is built up to it."

— JOHN BEALE BORDLEY, 1799

The massive stone walls of barns like the one on the Charles farm were kept from spreading by the rigidity of the interior frame. As was customary in Europe, these timbers were often secured to the walls by iron tiebacks, sometimes embellished with stars or other decorative exterior plates. The vertical slots in the wall, known as loopholes, provide ventilation and light. Support for the weight of the roof is supplied in part by interim purlins and a system of braces and struts. Braces this long are unusual. The loose hay gives a sense of the appearance of barns before the advent of hay baling.

below

Early settlers in southeastern Pennsylvania found the fertile valleys so thickly forested that their first task was undoubtedly clearing land for cultivation. The vast supply of high-quality timber, combined with the German tradition of log building, made notched-log construction an attractive alternative to labor-intensive timber framing. The 1798 tax records for Chester County alone list 598 log barns; most were small, averaging a relatively meager 739 square feet.

overleaf

As farms prospered and larger structures were needed, some of those log barns were enveloped by expanding buildings. Ordinarily, the log barns were completely disassembled and the hewn logs were used to make the members of larger, lighter timber frames. The Roher barn includes a number of heavy hewn mow poles with notching at one or both ends, betraying their origins. The shape of the original, smaller stone supporting wall is visible in the rear.

Nearly every farm in colonial America possessed some form of granary for the storage of threshed grain. Settlers so valued grain that they sometimes kept it in the attics of their houses. More commonly, it was stored in the loft over the combined wagon house–corncrib. In Pennsylvania barns, where stalls for livestock were relegated to the cellar, there was enough space near the threshing floor to provide a room to safeguard grain; the closed door leads to such a granary. The trapdoor in the foreground allowed the farmer to pitch meal or hay to the pens below.

"The granary was usually boarded off in one corner. Opening the door suddenly, there was apt to be a scampering of mice and rats. If the pet dogs of the family were the companions of the children, chase was given at once. At it they went, scattering the threshed grain upon the floor, tumbling down the wooden grainshovel and half-bushel measure, leaping over the wheat-bags ready for the mill, and sliding down great heaps of shelled corn, until the mischief was arrested by calling off the dogs and closing the doors, leaving these hunting grounds to those more careful hunters, the cats."

— GERTRUDE LEFFERTS VANDERBILT, 1882

82

The upland side of the barn at Springton Manor Farm in Chester County, Pennsylvania, presents an unassuming façade that belies the monumentality of the interior framing. The ventilating cupola became popular in the mid-nineteenth century. This late example is an alteration made to accommodate fashion as much as functionalism.

As exemplified at Springton Manor, the Pennsylvania barn followed a large rectangular plan, with the doors to the central threshing area placed on the upland (north) side. So popular was this arrangement that when a site failed to provide a south-facing slope, an earthen ramp was constructed to give access to the threshing floor. As livestock was consigned to the cellar, the vast upper barn was reserved primarily for threshing and storing hay. Employing indigenous oak, framing in the German tradition relied not on massive freestanding timbers but on complex interior bents. With so wide a roof, interim purlins were required on the rafters to spread the weight. Purlin struts in turn transfer the load to the lower frame.

"The cobwebs begrimed with dust, in tattered festoons, ornamented with hayseed, hanging from the beams; the horses stretching out their long noses from their stalls; the rough rope harness; the detached bits of wagons, board seats, tongue or shaft; the farming implements, the bags of grain, and beside them the iron-rimmed half bushel measure; the old knife or broken scythe stuck in the side of the barn; the black bucket of tar for the wagon wheels; the accounts chalked on the doors, and above all, the sweet smell of hay pervading the place — how these things come back to memory as we recall the old barns in the days when the village was tilled as farming lands!"

— GERTRUDE LEFFERTS VANDERBILT, 1882

opposite

The sheer capaciousness of the Springton Manor barn gives some notion of the wealth of hay harvested on a Pennsylvania farm in the mid-1800s. Properties in this region typically totaled three hundred acres of farmland — far more than in New England. The land was more fertile as well; crops were substantial, and the barns reflected this prosperity. Ladders framed into the interior bents were typical of Pennsylvania barns, and allowed farmhands forking up haymows from the floor to the rafters in the heat of summer to climb down for an occasional breath of fresh air.

By connecting farm buildings, a farmer could avoid trips outdoors in foul weather and at the same time block the winter winds, providing a protected barnyard for the animals. Another common plan includes buildings on three sides of the barnyard to form a U shape. Rarely is the yard enclosed on all four sides — an arrangement popular in Europe. Connections at right angles are far more common than the odd angles employed here in a complex in Erwinna, Pennsylvania. Gates and a high stone wall complete the enclosure.

The rambling barn of a working farm in Lancaster County illustrates many characteristics of the typical Pennsylvania barn of German-Swiss derivation. The massive stone walls rise all the way to the peak of the original structure. Visible just below the rake boards in the gable are the exposed butt ends of the plates and purlins. Ventilation is provided to the vast haymows through a series of loopholes. The cantilevered forebay, a defining feature of the Sweitzer barn, is clad in vertical boards on the south side. To the north a gambrel-roofed addition extends the threshing floor over wagon sheds. Built on a site with only a gentle grade, this barn required a stone-and-earth ramp to the elevated threshing floor.

The innovative interior of this Lancaster County barn discloses a surprising feature. The threshing floor is elevated a full story above the base of the haymow, forming a bridge. By driving a loaded wagon onto the bridge, the farmer could pitch hay down fairly easily. In such double-decker or three-level haybarns, the area immediately below the span was sometimes used as a tack room or granary.

"In these huge barns the cereal wealth of the farmer was stored. Reaping and threshing machines were not in use at the time . . . and the process of separating the wheat and chaff was more tedious than it is now.

"The grain to be threshed was spread in a circle upon the barn-floor. It was trodden out by the feet of the horses which were driven round and round upon it, the driver standing in the middle, and his assistants keeping with their wooden forks the grain in its position, if it happened to be displaced by the horses. Rye was threshed out by the flail, a sound that one never hears now; then on many an autumn or winter day, one might hear from the open barn door the regular thump! thump! thump! thump! of the flail as the farmer and his men threshed out the grain for winter use preparatory to taking it to the mill."

— GERTRUDE LEFFERTS VANDERBILT, 1882

Opening the large doors at the opposite ends of the threshing floor was important, not only for the light it gave the threshers but also for the draft, which aided the winnowing. Wind was channeled into the central breezeway, where it picked up the light, unwanted chaff but left the separated grain. In order to prevent any loose grain from being lost, farmers used an ingenious device that was first introduced in England and continental Europe. The jambs of the wagon doors were slotted at the bottom to allow the insertion of a board called a threshold — a term that has clearly outlived its agrarian origins. Abbreviated threshold boards remain in place in the eighteenth-century Oktoop barn near Halland, Sweden. At the English-style Van Dyke barn near Hopewell, New Jersey, the boards have long since been lost, but the slots survive.

In the Appalachian region, the threshold was
created by cutting a bevel out of the sill at the
door opening. Grain that landed on the sill during threshing or winnowing would slide back
onto the threshing floor.

Doors to the threshing floor were large — large enough to admit a fully loaded haywagon, to provide light in structures that originally had no windows, and to allow the air flow required for winnowing. In New World Dutch and English barns the opening was usually eleven or twelve feet square; in Pennsylvania it ranged up to fourteen or sixteen feet wide. On a daily basis, particularly in bad weather, smaller doors were sufficient for the farmer's needs. In barns of the Dutch and English tradition, low four- to five-foot-wide doors opened directly into the side bays where the animals were housed. These structures often included a small door for people beside the wagon entry. In New World Dutch barns, especially in New York State, one of the wagon doors was divided horizontally so people could open the lower half independently for their own use. But in Pennsylvania a common solution was to insert a door within a door.

Although most early barns were windowless, by the nineteenth century, when these Pennsylvania barns were constructed, windows were a standard feature. Since hay was stacked against the inside end walls, gable windows above the stable level typically appear only at the very top. Diamond-shaped brick vents in the stone gable ends allow air and additional light into the Lehigh Valley barn.

The Erwin-Stover barn, a landmark overlooking the Delaware River in Bucks County, is graced with a fanlight window high in the gable. Additional light and ventilation are supplied by the cupola. The vent on the side of the ramp indicates the presence of a root cellar inside. A vaulted cellar ceiling was required to handle the weight of the loaded haywagons that passed above.

The colorful geometric decorations of the Pennsylvania Dutch are known as hex signs. These symbols (often a star within a circle) are of European origin and adorn not only barnsides but furniture, pottery, and even tombstones. In Wallace Nutting's 1924 book *Pennsylvania Beautiful*, they are linked with mysticism: "The ornaments on barn foundations in Pennsylvania . . . go by the local name of hexfoos or witch foot. . . . They are supposed to be a continuance of very ancient tradition, according to which these decorative marks were potent to protect the barn, or more particularly the cattle, from the influences of witches." Later research suggests that instead of warding off evil, the hex signs used in Pennsylvania were purely decorative. This small stone barn has a forebay embellished with two swirling ornaments. The six-point star-within-a-star design includes crosses, scallops, and dots.

The forebay of the Pennsylvania barn varied widely according to local tradition and the prevalence of materials. The stucco-over-stone barn has projecting floor joists that support a shallow, fully cantilevered forebay boldly delineated in oxblood paint. Shuttered louvers and Dutch stable doors light the basement stalls. A frame barn with a closed-end forebay is clad in vertical siding and embellished with a fanciful bargeboard, which defines the roof edge of the gable. Fences embrace barnyards that are protected from winter winds by the slope of the land and the barns themselves.

The huge barn at Spring Hill Farm near New Hope, Pennsylvania, is remarkable for its great height and refined masonry. Typical of many Bucks County barns, it has a closed-end forebay, defined in this case by massive piers of dressed quoin stones. A block high on the gable wall proclaims the year of the raising as 1853. At the center of the wooden forebay are three tiers of paired doors; the middle set marks the level of the threshing floor, which bridges deep haymows. Between these "saddlebag" mows, below the threshing floor, is a granary. From the foundation to the peak of the gable, the stone walls rise more than fifty feet. Gathering the tens of thousands of requisite stones was a task no less awesome than actually laying up the walls.

The Old Order Amish are a strict sect of Mennonites who shun twentieth-century technologies such as electricity and gasoline engines in favor of traditional methods such as windmills and horse-drawn equipment. Since they do not use telephones or automobiles, the Amish need a tight settlement pattern to maintain their way of life. While Amish farming communities thrive in the South and Midwest, the largest concentration, east of Lancaster, Pennsylvania, is struggling for survival against the pressures of escalating land prices and busloads of tourists. One unusual Amish barn in this community employs a ramp to a door that projects from the top of the gable. This is a variation of the double-decker barn, which enables the farmer to pitch hay down to the haymows.

A Britisher, Thomas Anburey, suggested in 1789 that "the farmers in Pennsylvania and the Jerseys pay more attention to the construction of their barns than their dwelling houses. The building is nearly as large as a common country church." For the Amish, the barn sometimes *is* the country church. In order to avoid persecution in Europe for their religious beliefs, the Amish did not make use of church buildings but chose instead to worship in their homes. This tradition, like most Amish traditions, endures. In summer, services may be held in the barn on the threshing floor. John A. Hostetler described an Amish baptismal service: "The sun shone on the faces of the audience through the entrance of the large swinging doors. . . . The pure white aprons were saturated with water, and the fringes were soiled with the moisture and dirt of the barn floor. Overhead high on the inside of the barn, the pigeons were flapping their wings as they flew from one end of the barn to the other. A gentle breeze brought from the open door of the straw shed a cloud of fine particles of chaff and dust."

The barn at the Museum of Appalachia represents a building type unique to mountainous areas of North Carolina and Tennessee. Known as the cantilever barn, it was brought to the region by postrevolutionary migrants moving inland along the Appalachians from Pennsylvania, and it may be based in part on Swiss and German houses with overhanging upper floors and outbuildings. The supporting log cribs, generally measuring about twelve to eighteen feet, were typically used for crop storage. The distinctive element lay above, in the spacious cantilevered lofts. To achieve this form, the builders extended the top logs along the crib wall parallel to the ridge so they would support a series of cantilevered logs, which stretched the full width of the loft. Projecting on all sides eight to twelve feet beyond the cribs, the loft walls were usually built with a timber frame, including queen post trusses and continuous purlins and plates. Sheathing was of weatherboard, roofing of boards or shingles. The corner joints of the log cribs were variously notched. The half-dovetail was most popular, but square notching, saddle notching, and V notching, as illustrated, were also employed.

Because of the rockiness of the soil, the ready availability of saplings, and the transient nature of early settlement, snake fences, which required no posthole digging, became the dominant regional form of enclosure.

The Enloe barn was built in the mid-nineteenth century at Floyd Bottoms on the Oconaluftee River in the Great Smoky Mountains of North Carolina. The raw texture and straightforward geometry of its exterior disguise the structural integrity inside. Central to the framework are two elongated log pens or cribs, which run parallel to the ridge of the roof and flank a central driveway. This configuration, also seen in houses in the region, is known as a dogtrot. Early cribs were used as granaries for wheat and rye as often as corn, but here enclosed a string of stalls. Some double-pen barns in the area support a fully cantilevered structure with a wide overhang on all four sides. In the Enloe barn, much of the weight of the logs is borne by an enclosure of outside posts. The band of wooden-slat louvers at the eaves served to ventilate the haymow and to prevent fires caused by spontaneous combustion.

The tie-up of the Enloe barn frames a solitary horse where once all the farm's cows were sheltered. Mules and horses were generally housed apart from cows. Far larger than most double-pen structures in the area, the Enloe barn complemented the large farm it was built to serve. In 1849 Wesley Enloe had two hundred of his five hundred acres under cultivation; his livestock included eight horses, twelve milk cows, twenty-four beef cattle, fifteen sheep, and sixty hogs. The Oconaluftee Turnpike, chartered in 1832, passed through the Enloe Farm on its way along the Indian Gap Trail through the mountains to North Carolina. Vast numbers of cattle and hogs were driven along the route, and barns like the one at Floyd Bottoms were known locally as drovers' barns. Farmers driving livestock to market would often keep their herds under the sheltered tie-ups overnight, providing the host farmer in return with a much-appreciated premium for any feed or fuss.

Although English barn types were known in seaboard settlements of the South, the influence of that tradition was limited. Rather, the immigration of Germans and Scotch-Irish from Pennsylvania provided the upland South with the inspiration for both notched-log and timber-frame structures. Still, new forms developed because of differences in cultivated crops and climate. Because winters were mild, animals were sheltered on open sheds rather than enclosed stalls. Harvests required protection, but a major

crop in the South, tobacco, called for barns with extremely good ventilation. In any event, southern barns were smaller than Pennsylvania barns, as exemplified by the Booker T. Washington homestead in Virginia. Under a broad half-hip roof of split oak, the one-story structure encompasses a side-aisle wagon driveway and an area devoted to the mow. The frame itself is light, and many members, such as the rafters, are undressed sapling poles.

Built in Botetourt County, Virginia, during the decade preceding the Civil War, the Barger barn is another example of a double-pen log barn. Between the pens, which serve as mow and granary, is a heavy-boarded threshing floor rather than an open driveway. The boxlike pens support a series of long cantilevered timbers, which extend out in all directions to carry a wraparound shed roof under which livestock could be sheltered. In keeping with contemporary practice, the roof forms a comb at the ridge where shingles on the windward face project a few inches over the peak. The Barger barn has been restored as a part of the Museum of American Frontier Culture in Staunton, Virginia.

The true measure of a farmer's diligence was the bounty of harvested hay pitched into mows from floor to rafters in his barn. In the full heat of summer, farmhands forked seemingly endless wagonloads higher and higher until they found themselves twenty or even thirty feet above the floor. Barn builders devised many ways for workers to climb down. In southeastern Pennsylvania, ladders were framed into the complex bents on each side of the threshing floor. Barns throughout the Northeast sometimes included a series of holes drilled into central posts, through which framers could run rungs to form a single-pole ladder. One New World Dutch barn, now destroyed, sported a similar series of rungs that spiraled around an arcade post. In an Anglo-Dutch barn, well-worn hand- and footholds are pocketed into the horizontal boards, called breast boards, that hold the hay in the mow. In addition to having ladders, many barns contained a hay chute, an open shaft about four feet square through which hay could be dropped directly to the stables below.

It is unknown whether the carved capital on the short post that supports the center of the tie beam of this eighteenth-century English-style barn in Bucks County, Pennsylvania, had some function, or whether it is purely ornamental. The rough-textured tie beam is oak, while the carved post is poplar. The hole is one of six that once held rungs that formed a ladder.

"There were beams across the second story, supporting poles on which the hay was piled. What great haymows they were, choice romping places for children! Just the spot to hunt for hens' nests, or from which to jump to the soft bedding of hay thrown down on the lower floor! And then what boisterous laughter followed the leap, as the frolicsome little ones were almost buried by the downward plunge into the fragrant clover hay! . . . If by mistake they frightened a setting hen from her nest, what a noisy cackling was heard, followed by the unnecessary advice from some of the farm-hands to 'let that hen alone!' "

— GERTRUDE LEFFERTS VANDERBILT, 1882

"But a barn is also a cathedral where visiting town-boys come to worship farm life. It has the well-rubbed wood of a reverenced church rail, the grain raised by the protruberant hides of quietly agnostic cows. In the hayloft you learn the meaning of motes and beams. You walk across its plank floor, head tilted back. Day outside finds cracks in the roof and walls of the hayloft, and light streaks through the darkness on missions of grace and accusation. The barn is wired to God's wrath by a lightning rod."

— VERLYN KLINKENBORG, 1986

The trotting horse adorns a barn door in Cookesburg, New York, and a black cockerel struts against barn red in Stanton, New Jersey.

Some barns have no graffiti inside, while others are covered with it. A single inscription or set of initials on a board partition, it seems, can often unleash an outpouring of messages. Names and dates are common, but although they occasionally acknowledge the builder and date of construction, they are far more likely the result of idle carving. Hex signs, sayings, and drawings are sometimes found scratched into breast boards, as are Roman numerals, which may have been counts of wagonloads of hay.

On one door riotously autographed by farmhands, the apparently unimpressed farmer, named Van Marter, left his own neatly inscribed statement: "Fools names, like fools faces, Always found in public places."

In less prosperous farming regions, particularly mountainous areas, painting barns was a low priority, as evidenced by the large numbers of barns clad with natural, weathered board siding. However, a farmer could get a free paint job by allowing a producer to promote a product on his barn. The advertiser might be a local firm pitching anything from insurance to tires or a national company touting the merits of chewing tobacco.

"Down the road from us in Cedar Grove a man lived by the name of Morris Maple. And they called him Doc Maple. One of his relatives left him the recipe for making liniment and cough syrup and all that sort of thing. And for years he made cough syrup, liniment, cough drops. All the way down the road there were cherry trees just hanging with wild cherries, and he used them for flavor. He also put up vaseline, castor oil, toothache drops. He had a horse and wagon and he'd load up and drive all over Jersey supplying drugstores. And he would go to a farmer and say, 'Look, I'll paint the gable of your barn if you'll let me put my advertising there.' And for years and years after he died you could go around the country and see barns with 'Maple's Electric Liniment.'"

— ELMER H. LEIGH, 1971

A close look at Pennsylvania barns reveals some delightful details. The inventive semicircular door hinges on a double barn near Newburg in the Lehigh Valley are still working, although the idea apparently never caught on. Frequently, strap hinges were carefully wrought into fanciful designs, such as these hinges on a door within a door. The weight of a large hay door meant that the strap hinge had to pivot on a pintle that was driven deep into the oak doorjamb.

Hearts and tulips were favorite motifs in Pennsylvania, not just for hardware. Martin holes cut into the siding at the top of a barn gable provide ventilation as well as decoration.

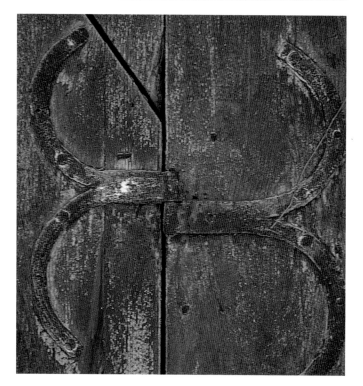

Throughout Pennsylvania's central and south-eastern counties, and in the nearby Maryland countryside, some barns built of local brick have robust and rhythmic designs in their gable ends. In the 1798 Pennsylvania tax survey, only ten brick barns were chronicled. But in the decades that followed, as settlers' primitive structures were superseded by larger barns, many prosperous farmers in areas with soil rich in clay opted for brick. Apparently brickmakers journeyed to these farms to quarry the clay and fire the brick on site. When limestone was available locally, it too was gathered and burned in the makeshift kilns to create lime for mortar. Bricks were laid up in common or in flemish bond patterns, at times reaching a thickness of sixteen inches in the towering gable walls. Designs were created by omitting alternate headers to form ventilation holes. In order to maintain the intrinsic strength of the construction, the number and diversity of the designs were limited. Most were geometric rectangles, triangles, and diamonds arranged to form stars, hourglasses, wineglasses, wheat sheaves, or fir trees. These motifs were repeated in vertical and horizontal patterns. In a few instances farmers' initials were picked out; one notable example displays a top-hatted man on a mule. Such festive vents exhibit an unselfconscious harmony of beauty and practicality.

The barn on the Roher family farm west of Lancaster is an example of the adaptation of the Pennsylvania barn for tobacco storage. Because the curing process required a great deal of ventilation, almost half the horizontal sheathing is composed of louvers, which can be opened like blinds with long poles. Inside, the tobacco leaves were suspended from undressed saplings spanning the bays in tiers from floor to rafters.

The juxtaposition of greatly enlarged dairy barns and mighty silos in American barnyards reflects the development of year-round milking after the Civil War, when the enormous increase in demand for milk in the burgeoning cities led to a change in agricultural emphasis in surrounding rural areas. Morning and evening milking became the parentheses of daily life on the farm. Nostalgia aside, for those who practiced this tedious operation by hand, memories are not always sweet.

"It is quite surprising how many people from outside agriculture imagine that milking by hand is enjoyable and clean. They carry an image of fresh-faced milkmaids in the open air sitting on three-legged stools. . . . It was not like that at all. Cows are just about the most filthy animals you can imagine, and when you were milking by hand, within minutes of commencing work, you too were filthy. Cows brought in from the fields in winter are plastered with mud. You had to do your best to get this off them and particularly off their udders to try to keep the milk reasonably clean. . . . That immediately made the cow-

shed absolutely filthy and you sat in the filth, milking by hand, while they fidgeted and flipped you in the face with their tails, which were also soon dirty. They occasionally kicked you quite hard with their filthy feet and maybe even knocked you over in the muck. In fact, there was no job more conducive to ill temper and misery in the early morning than fetching in a lot of cows in cold weather when, maybe, you had to go quite a distance in the mud to fetch them and then had to sit down under them to milk them by hand."

— TONY HARMAN, 1986

"In the days not so long ago when all farmers milked and the white glazed-brick creameries in small towns had not closed and milk tanktrucks still toured the rural routes, there were, as everyone knows, two lively times in the day of a barn — morning and evening, when cows wandered up from pasture for some artificial nursing; swishing of milkers, slap of hooves, flopping of manure, clank of head-gates, the rasping of an old bakelite radio (that goes on with the lights) set high on the wall between the joists."

— VERLYN KLINKENBORG, 1986

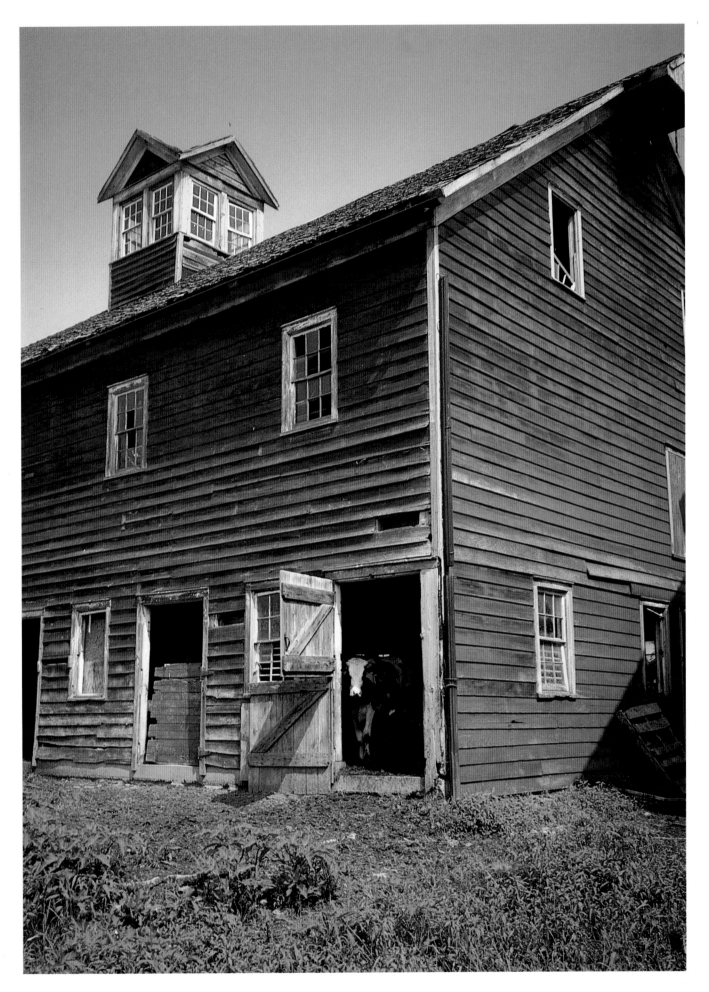

Not all cupolas were erected solely for the obvious benefits of increased light and ventilation. Crowning the dominant structure of a gentleman farmer's estate, they also served to convey his sophistication. One example at Mount Rose, New Jersey, was a local landmark:

"The Jacksons had a wonderful big barn. And that barn had a cupola on it that was a good size — probably ten feet square. It was a room really. It had windows on all sides of it, and there was a stairway that led up to it. And all the guests when they visited there rushed over to that cupola. And the whole wall all the way round between the windows, or wherever you could find space, was signatures where guests had signed. You had a view all the way round. You could look across the valley and see the Reading Railroad with the

trains coming back and forth. But then there was a very severe windstorm come along and destroyed that whole barn."

The age of the self-sufficient American farm drew to an end in the nineteenth century, when a vast portion of the country's rural population emigrated to the newly industrialized cities. With the development of canals, roads, and railroads, farms were closer to this new market. Consequently, successful landowners replaced smaller and simpler structures with grand, commodious barns embellished with decorative devices. Cupolas, often in rhythmic multiples, might have been justified in practical terms, but no one doubted their ability to turn the eye as well, particularly when they were dressed with gingerbread brackets and a splendid weather vane.

112

Descended from medieval heraldic banners known as fanes, which adorned rooftops, weather vanes swivel according to the direction of the wind. Early American churches and public buildings were frequently topped with elaborate vanes, often gilded. Farmers, who needed to read the weather daily, placed their own, sometimes highly original versions on their barns. Locally fashioned weather vanes of wood, iron, and copper eventually gave way to mass-produced examples. Animal motifs, especially cows, horses, and pigs, were most popular.

"Upon the peak was a lively weather-cock of shingle, most preposterously active in its motions, and trimming to every flaw of wind with a nervous rapidity, that reminded me of nothing so much as the alacrity of a small newspaper editor."

— ISAAK MARVEL, 1863

Beginning in the mid-1800s the American barn was transformed. Larger barns, often incorporating functions previously included in several farm structures, were constructed. As local forests were depleted and railroads came to link the far reaches of the nation, softwood beams sawed to standard dimensions and shipped by rail often replaced indigenous hardwood in timber framing. By the end of the century, timber-frame technology was largely eclipsed by stick-frame construction, in which heavy, pegged post-and-beam sections were replaced with light studded walls and trussed roofs. This innovation was one of many suggested by popular agricultural journals, which included articles on all aspects of land and crop development, husbandry, farm construction, and home crafts, and inspirational if mawkish fiction. Among the barn improve-ments put forward were sliding doors, manure trolleys, flexible stanchions, hay carriers, silos, cupolas, ventilators, lightning rods, and weather vanes. By 1900 application of the principles of the industrial revolution made barn construction more practical and economical, but at the price of local diversity.

Ventilation was touted as an essential element in barn design, not only to prevent fires caused by spontaneous combustion in the mow but to foster healthful and hygienic conditions in the basement animal areas. Early examples took the form of louvered cupolas, but journals and farm supply catalogues subsequently introduced more sophis-ticated systems in which wind-driven rotors on the roof drew air through ducts throughout the barn.

"But if hay was down when it rained, I was as gloomy as anyone. The stacks had to be torn apart and the hay spread to dry, and then turned over to dry on the other side, and then stacked again. Sometimes we would just finish stacking the hay a second time when a thundershower would soak it again. If it was three times wet, even the best hay turned into a mud-colored and odorless straw. We would either throw it away or pass it off on the poor sheep."

— DONALD HALL, 1983

"The weather was always a prime consideration because once the hay was cut and had begun to dry, rain could make many problems. Occasionally the weather clouded up, forming what Pop called 'bullheads.' If we were in the midst of gathering hay that was already dry, the efforts would be redoubled to get as much of it on the wagon as possible before the rain struck. When the storms threatened, the horses were always nervous and wanted to head back to the barn."

— F. M. UPDIKE, 1981

The roofs of most early barns formed a traditional triangular gable. As farms grew in size and
more hay was needed for greater numbers of
livestock, one way to increase the loft capacity
was to substitute a gambrel roof, distinguished
by two slopes, one gentle, one steep. The word
gambrel comes from a word for the hock or hind
leg of a horse, which is roughly the same shape as
half the profile of the roof. Rare on barns before
the middle of the nineteenth century, gambrel
roofs became extremely popular after they were
endorsed by agricultural journals and books on
progressive farming. Some farmers went so
far as to remove a gable roof and replace it with
a gambrel.

The large barn with the porch entry is in Lancaster County, Pennsylvania. On a few gambrel
roofs, as on the Clinton, New Jersey, barn, the
break in the roofline occurs close to the ridge.
The same roof form graces some of the early
Dutch colonial houses found in that area, and
has survived in the typical Dutch colonial design
so familiar in suburban America.

As the nineteenth century drew to a close, the American farm was changed most dramatically by the introduction of the silo. In 1875, the *American Agriculturist*, a farm journal printed in both English and German, introduced pit silos, trenches into which green crops were pitched, closed off from the air, and stored for fodder. After the upright or raised silo became popular, pit silos proved awkward. Some early silos were square, but the tall round silo emerged as the most efficient and enduring design.

The favored silage crop was corn, which had a high nutritional value. Ears, husks, and stalks were chopped up by a feed cutter and blown through a pipe into the top of the silo, and sometimes tamped down by foot. The weight of the silage and the tamping down pressed out the air. Cows that were fed on this green silage in the winter gave milk year round, and the resulting boost in profits led many farmers to increase the size of their herds. Despite some initial opposition, by the turn of the century the silo was firmly established, with nearly half a million in place, primarily in the Northeast.

Some silos are constructed of tongue-and-groove boards, or staves, secured by bands fastened with turnbuckles. Today, after decades of exposure, some are listing away from the prevailing winds, and many have collapsed. Other silos are built of concrete, stone, brick, terra cotta, and, recently, a combination of metal and fiberglass.

opposite

Another piece of farm apparatus introduced by agricultural journals was a manure carrier, which traveled on a track behind the cow stalls and out a door in the dairy barn. According to the Jamesway catalogue of 1921, "The big tub of the Jamesway carrier holds as much as three or four wheelbarrow loads; the carrier can be run out and dumped in less time than a single wheelbarrow. The saving of time and work is very large."

pulled to the end of the track, it would trip and the hay fork could be pulled down to the load. We used a 'harpoon' fork. This looked like an inverted 'U' with the two legs about three feet long. These were pushed down into the load. When they were properly positioned, two prongs which were recessed in the legs would be engaged, so that when the fork was pulled up, a really large amount of hay would be carried up to the track and along that to the proper place in the barn. This was accomplished by a series of ropes and pulleys. The other end of the rope was led out to the ground at the opposite end of the barn and the power to raise the hay was provided by a team of horses. . . . When the trip rope was pulled, the prongs recessed into the tines (or legs) and the hay slid off. There were other types of hay forks, such as the grapple fork, but all of them operated on essentially the same principle. . . .

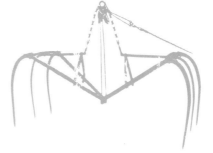

"When the fork was properly placed and everything was ready to hoist it into the barn, the man on the wagon would yell 'go ahead.' That was the signal to start the horses and pull up the fork. Then, when it was pulled along to the proper place in the mow, the men in the barn would yell 'whoa.' . . . Mom always claimed that her days during haying were filled with the shouts of 'go ahead' and 'whoa.' "

— F. M. UPDIKE, 1981

"Each of the hay mows had a hay track. This was a metal rail suspended at the peak of the barn. Along this track a little trolley or crane could move the entire length of the barn. This carried the "hay fork," a device for unloading the hay. At one end of each of the hay barns was a large mow door which could be swung open. The track extended for approximately three feet beyond the side of the barn. When the trolley was

"No door is so convenient for barns, or stables, as one that is hung upon rollers, and can be pushed to one side, occupying practically no space, and being entirely out of the way. Such doors cannot blow shut, or open, as hinged doors will do in gusty days, to the ruin of the hinges, if not of the doors themselves, and frequently to the injury of the farm animals which may be in the vicinity."

— AMERICAN AGRICULTURIST, 1876

Although round and polygonal barns did not become popular in America until late in the 1800s, earlier isolated examples were known on gentlemen's show farms. In 1793 George Washington designed and built a sixteen-sided structure for his Dogue Run Farm in Fairfax County, Virginia. It proved something of a practical disappointment, owing, it seems, to "the almost impossibility of putting overseers of this country out of the track they have been accustomed to walk in."

Far-flung fame attended the round barn raised in 1824 by the Shaker community at Hancock, Massachusetts. A contemporary agricultural journal found its innovations "worthy of the attention of farmers who are contemplating the erection of barns upon a large scale. . . . The barn is [90] feet in diameter, built of stone. . . . It is two stories high, . . . and contains stalls for 52 head of cattle. . . . The stalls are situated in a circle next to the outer wall, with the heads of the animals pointing . . . into the alley. . . . The circle forming the stable and alleyway is 14 feet wide, inside of which is a great bay [measuring 55 feet across]. Over the stable and alley is the threshing floor, which [again] is 14 feet wide, and about 300 feet long on the outer side, into which a dozen loads of hay may be hauled and all unloaded at the same time into the bay at the center [to a depth of 30 feet]."

By mid-century a national craze for octagonal houses was fostered by a phrenologist named Orson S. Fowler. His predilection for the healthful powers of polygonal structures included barns. Writing in 1853, he claimed, "In [barns] especially we need some common *center* in and around which to work. This form will turn heads of all the horses and cattle, and openings to all the bays and bins toward the center, so that one can pass from bay to stall . . . with half the steps required in a square [barn]. . . . It will allow you to . . . drive a wagon and cart around in a circle. . . . It also furnishes just the shaped floor required for [circular] threshing with horses."

Noted agriculturists Elliott W. Stewart and Lorenzo S. Coffin disseminated actual plans for octagonal barns through farming journals, and by the 1880s hundreds had been built, most employing timber frames. Similarly, round barns with balloon frames were built across America in the first decades of the twentieth century before the style was finally abandoned.

In prosperous farming regions, barns were commonly enlarged with connecting sheds and ells, despite the danger of the spread of fire. Dairy barns, stables, wagon houses, equipment sheds, and milk houses were added, either as separate buildings or as additions to the old hay barn. A forebay barn in Warren County, New Jersey, sprouted ells in two different directions. A low modern dairy barn has been added to an already sprawling farm complex in New England.

"Farm laborers receive fully double the wages, except at harvest time, that they did fifty years ago; therefore the barns should be planned with the view of economizing labor. This can best be secured by rearing a single structure, rather than several, for it is evident that if the livestock, tools, implements and provender be placed in juxtaposition, economy in performing the work of the [farm] will be secured."

— ISAAC PHILLIPS ROBERTS, c. 1900

A connected farm in Standish, Maine, forms an L shape. At the Norlands Living History Farm in Livermore Falls, Maine, the kitchen ell (little house) is connected directly to the main barn.

In parts of New England, particularly southern Maine and New Hampshire, the notion of connecting farm structures did not stop with the outbuildings. Thomas Hubka, quoting a children's rhyme, describes this string of farm buildings as "big house, little house, back house, [and] barn." The little house was the kitchen ell, which often included a workroom and woodshed, and the back house served as a wagon house,

work area, and storage space. Typically the privy was in a corner of this section. When the connected-farm plan became a symbol of progressive farm organization in the middle of the nineteenth century, preexisting detached outbuildings were frequently uprooted and moved into the new alignment. The line of buildings was either straight or staggered and extended to the rear or the side of the big house. The connected farm provided protection from winter winds and eliminated the need to venture outdoors in bad weather to perform chores. Perhaps just as important, this layout brought farm tasks into a labor-saving proximity and satisfied a need for order.

Red-painted barns are common in Norway, Sweden, and North America. Traditionally, this attractive color is the result of farmers' protecting their weatherboards with a mixture of red oxide from their soil, linseed oil from their flax crop, and casein from the milk of their cows.

William K. Sladcik, from Illinois, has traveled the back roads of the Midwest to photograph working barns and those that are no longer the center of farming activity.

Dixon, Illinois

Illinois-Wisconsin border

Iowa

Southern Wisconsin

Raising

TODAY, few people have felt the pleasure of driving home a peg to secure a precisely chiseled mortise-and-tenon joint, or of helping a company of able and eager neighbors raise a giant bent from its horizontal assembly position to its mighty stance as the bulwark of a barn. But these experiences led to the most enduring quality with which early builders endowed their barns: integrity. Whether considering materials, design, tools, or procedures, these men approached their task straightforwardly, economically, chastely.

Indigenous materials literally matched the landscape from which they were wrested. Stones that challenged tillage were gathered and laid up into foundations, ramps, and whole barns. These walls were cemented with native clay bonded with straw and animal hair. In areas where the soil was red with clay, simple pits and kilns produced the hundreds of thousands of bricks it took to build structures in harmony with the fields around them. As a Cistercian builder is said to have remarked, "Beauty is the child of necessity."

The same was true of the forest. Settlers often left as much as a third of their land — the acreage that would prove hardest to till, because of wetlands or slopes — in woods, reserving it to supply future generations with timber, fuel, and game. As they cleared the remaining land for cultivation, they set aside choice hardwoods such as oak for construction. When they girdled or cut these trees, they prudently allowed several years to pass so the trunks could cure before they were fashioned into timbers.

Perhaps it was during this period that a farmer or his framer set down a plan for the barn and other outbuildings. While these designs generally followed cultural precedent, there was no room for superficiality. Every structural member performed a specific function: the stoutest were selected to carry great weight over wide spans; the longest were reserved for plates or purlins running the length of the structure.

The same economy determined the somewhat specialized tools used to construct a barn. The broad axe and adze were preferred for hewing logs square. Although these tools required skill, strength, and endurance to use, the builders did not hack into the faces of the logs but swung the tools evenly, with the delicate touch of men whose handiwork was their gift to succeeding generations.

Dimensions for the frame were scribed onto a story pole, a long stick that was used to locate the timber joints. Where mortises were called for, scribe marks were transferred to the timbers. The carpenter then sank a series of interlocking holes with an auger and squared them by striking a chisel with a wooden mallet. Tenons too were dressed and beveled to ease their eventual insertion. The joints were designated with chiseled markings. Although each barn frame is individual, there is surprising uniformity in the size of mortises, tenons, braces, and pegs.

The master carpenter, the farmer, and a small complement of sons and farmhands might labor for many weeks to prepare the full inventory of timbers, but when it came time for raising the barn, the strength of many bodies was essential. And so of necessity barn raising became a vital tradition in American community life.

The raising day was as eagerly anticipated as a wedding. Here was an opportunity to visit and gossip even as one toiled. Before the dew had evaporated, farming families converged, the women to add their pots of beans or pies to the noontime groaning board, the men to examine the foundation — already bearing the sill plates and perhaps the floor — and the stacks of dressed and numbered timbers. Together the men carried the stoutest timbers for the first section, slipping designated tenons into mortises and pounding home pegs with sturdy wooden sledges.

Once the full assembly was readied and squared, the master carpenter called the company together. Men assumed positions around the bent. If they were using a gin pole rigged with a block and tackle, others would handle the ropes, which assisted in lifting the frame. In harmony, on "Heave-ho-hee," all backs and biceps tensed, tested the weight, and lifted the assembly the height of a forearm. Another "Heave-ho," and it stood as high as arms could reach. Then, one by one, pike poles were jabbed into the frame and pushed higher and higher with each successive directive. At last the first bent stood erect, casting long morning shadows over the satisfied participants. By the time the midday sun hung over the community of workmen, three or four more bents would have been rigged, raised, and secured with girts to one another.

After a welcome rest and a generous meal, the men returned to raise the plates, purlins, and rafters. According to custom, after the last set of rafters was placed, an evergreen branch was attached to the structure in a "topping out" ceremony. When the day's work was finished, the company relaxed, holding wrestling matches and observing traditions such as running the ridgepole. Drinks flowed, a feast was served, and then fiddlers started the dancing. Finally, weary but exhilarated by a sense of accomplishment, the participants drove home, having shared in a special event they would recall for a lifetime.

The barn builder took pride in his tools and wielded them with great skill. Most are large-scale versions of the tools of a carpenter. Cutting tools were sharpened fastidiously. On the right is the broad axe, which was honed to a chisel edge for hewing or squaring logs. Once the beams were shaped, mortises were laid out to be cut. The bulk of the mortise was removed by drilling a series of holes with the auger. The forming chisel was used next, to cut away additional debris in the mortise hole and square the corners. A larger version, the framing chisel, shaped the tenons. Both chisels were designed to be struck with a mallet, the head of which was generally the burl of a hardwood tree such as a beech or walnut. A common lumbering tool, the cant hook, was effective for rolling beams about. The leverage it provided was also useful for twisting beams while assembling bents. The wing compass was one of several layout tools. Much of the layout was done with the aid of a story pole, a long stick with scribe marks scratched onto the surface at all the necessary points of measurement. The beetle, or commander, was a heavy wooden sledgehammer useful for persuading reluctant joints to close. To smooth a rough surface, the barn builder relied on a huge chisel called a slick. This was pushed with the hands, never struck with a mallet.

135

SEVERAL YEARS AGO, as part of an effort to gather a more accurate group of early structures, the restored nineteenth-century town of Old Sturbridge Village in Massachusetts opted to provide its eighteenth-century Fenno House with a suitable and complementary barn of appropriate age, moderate proportions, and clearly documented generational growth. A survey of regional barns identified only a handful of eighteenth-century examples. From these, a deteriorating structure in New Braintree, Massachusetts, was selected.

Part of a farm settled in 1753, the chosen barn is mentioned in a 1767 inventory. Although built some forty years after Fenno House, it is comparable to barns of the early 1700s. Its hewn chestnut frame, measuring twenty-eight by thirty-two feet, includes gunstock corner posts and a roof of principal rafters supporting a series of purlins. At one time in its long history the barn was moved intact across the road from its original location, but it was not available for a move to Sturbridge. Instead, it was fully measured, drawn, and documented, and over a period of years Village carpenters replicated every timber in white oak.

In September 1988 a company of costumed members of the community gathered to raise the barn by the Fenno homestead. The tools and procedures they used were the traditional ones, documented in the following pages by statements collected during an oral history project and in a pamphlet titled "Of Purlins and Plates," published by the Early Trade and Crafts Society and the Friends of the Nassau County Museum, Long Island, New York. Although some raising traditions were universal, others were certainly local or regional and changed over time.

Long after settlers cleared farm lots and raised rude structures from felled timber, the construction of a new barn remained a process in which the farmer expected to provide most of the labor himself. As late as 1870, *The Agriculturalist* reported that "plain farmer folks . . . want plain barns, and they want to do about two-thirds of the work themselves. They will dig and lay the foundation, cut the timber, and haul it to and from the mill; with the aid of a carpenter, plan the frame, and see that they have the right stuff. They will spend winter evenings hewing treenails, and planning conveniences, and when Spring comes are ready to go-a-head, having a raising and shortly a barn."

However, as a New Englander named Alice Steele recalled, landowners were quick to acknowledge the particular skills of professionals within their developing communities:

"The farmer sought out an experienced carpenter, telling him the size and shape building desired, and the carpenter drew his own plans, gave the farmer a list of the size logs to be cut, and friends, neighbors, and relatives formed a bee and cut the necessary lumber from the farmer's own wood lot."

While the requisite timber was being felled, cured, and hauled to the site, the carpenter prepared the framing plans. Although early framers probably worked from nothing more than a basic floor plan and a materials list, occasionally the planning was more involved. Paul Wilson described the design process for a barn near Sylmar, Maryland:

"About 1919 my grandfather . . . commissioned Job Sidwell to draw the specifications. My father remembers the day this master builder . . . drove up in his buggy with the papers. They contained both plan view and elevations and went into great detail. When asked how much his trouble was worth, Mr. Sidwell replied that his trouble was worth two dollars and fifty cents."

With a design in hand, the farmer went about preparing the site. An area was selected at an appropriate distance from the house, suitably oriented to the sun and the prevailing wind. According to John Stilgoe, the author of *Common Landscapes of America, 1580 to 1845,* the dimensions of the barn were transposed from plan to ground by using an ancient and cleverly simple device:

"Every builder understood the folk 'ground rules' of making perfectly square or rectangular subassemblies and cellar holes. Using only a long rope and a peg, a builder first inscribed a circle on the ground, using the peg as the center point and the rope as a radius; then he stretched the rope at a tangent to the circle drawn in the dirt, scratched a line following the rope, then pivoted the rope about one of its ends until it again touched the circumference of the circle, making a perfect ninety-degree angle. By knotting the rope and varying it in length, a man totally ignorant of mathematics could produce a few rectilinear shapes as perfect as any grid line run by a federal surveyor."

In western Massachusetts, where Alice Steele grew up, Pennsylvania barns with mighty stone walls were virtually unknown before the second quarter of the nineteenth century, when cellars for manure storage were introduced by agricultural journals. Before then, barns were typically raised on a low foundation called an underpinning to forestall rot and frost heaving.

"While the carpenter was hewing the timber, cutting the mortises and tenons, and spotting the rafters and floor joists, the farmer dug the cellar with a pair of horses and a hill digger or sidehill scoop, and with the aid of a local, experienced stonemason laid a stone wall foundation to receive the barn sills. Those old foundation walls, often spoken of as dry stone walls, were laid without cement or anything except their own shape and size to keep them in place."

Meanwhile, the carpenter culled the pile of lumber and selected the best logs for each member.

"The sills, plates, and corner posts were hand hewn, square-cornered timbers, usually of either spruce or hemlock because these woods were readily available."

Mary Elizabeth Rogers describes the same barn-raising process in Aroostook, Maine:

"About 1845, Grandfather built the new barn. He hired men to prepare the frame. They hewed the big timbers until they were squared to the proper dimensions for the foundations, uprights, and great beams to hold the roof. Then they were mortised at . . . the proper places to insert the cross pieces and braces. Lastly, the rafters and ridgepole were cut and piled ready to be quickly used without confusion. Finally wooden pins were made to fasten the frame together."

An eighty-three-year-old carpenter recounted how some barn builders avoided confusion as the inventory of hewn and mortised timber grew:

"Sometimes names were written on the various pieces with chalk, together with the direction: north, south, east, or west."

Another common way to code timbers was to chisel characters and Roman numerals into adjoining timbers next to their joints.

The marks of joining. From the earliest days, beams, posts, and braces were identified with Roman numerals before assembly. These inscriptions can be found on many main timbers of old European and New World barns.

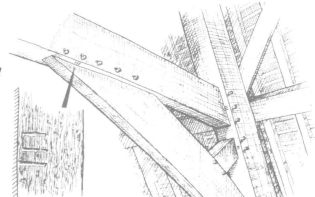

Elliot M. Sayward described a tool used by carpenters preparing barn beams:

"The 'story pole' was a measuring staff made especially for the job of framing the barn or other building. Its length was a divisor of each of the building's three dimensions — length, width, and height. With it, the carpenter could lay out any timber as measuring so many story poles in length. On the pole, marked by notched rings, were the depth and breadth of all the timbers to guide the hewers in shaping them."

As Alice Steele noted, not all timbers were hewn and squared:

"Then for rafters and floor joists, small straight trees of uniform size were selected and cut the proper length. The bark was then peeled off and they were spotted with an axe and adze to straighten one side only, so as to have a surface to nail the roof and floor boards to. This method was easier and cheaper than taking the logs to the sawmill and having them squared."

When the labor of fashioning the framing members was mostly finished, the carpenter, the farmer, and the hands lifted the sill plates into position on the foundation walls. Writing of a barn raising in Maine, Ralph Moody detailed the process that followed:

"Next [the carpenter] mortised the floor joists into the struts and sills. They weren't hewn square, as the other timbers were, but after all were mortised solidly in place, he adzed the rounded tops, so that anyone could sight across the whole floor frame without finding a single hump or hollow."

Once the floor was in place, the time had arrived to set a date and invite the neighbors. The Reverend Elijah Kellogg wrote of one final detail before the great day:

"The rest of the time was occupied in making long poles, with an iron in the end, to push the frame up with, when it was out of reach of the hand. They were of large size that a number of men might lift with them at once."

According to John Burroughs, the renowned naturalist,

"When the hands arrived, the great beams and posts and joists and braces were carried to their place on the platform, and the first bent was put together and pinned by the oak pins that the boys brought."

Vermonter Walter Needham related how his grandfather fashioned the pegs, or treenails, as they were called:

"When Gramp was whittling the white-oak pins they had to be a little bit off, and fit tight, or they wouldn't hold. Gramp originally whittled out or split out the pins by hand, but later on he made a steel ring that he could just drive a pin through, and that would shape it as near as he wanted."

As Anne Gertrude Sneller recalled from a raising in her youth in Onandaga County, New York, assembling bents served as a test of the carpenters' skills:

"The bents or sections were constructed and fitted together while lying flat on the ground; and every groove and pin was accounted for and ready, if the carpenters had done their work right, to slip into its appointed place."

Once the bent was assembled, the actual raising began.

"When the moment came for lifting the first bent from the ground, a line of men took their places before the heavy beams. Pike poles could not be used till after the bent was high enough up in the air so that poles could be slipped under it. Pike poles were long or short according to the height needed, with a sharp steel tip. The head carpenter was usually chosen leader to give the signals, for he knew best how all must pull together, and his keen eye could see in an instant any slackening in the line before the right height was reached. A last survey — then he waved his arms and shouted 'He-oh-heave.' With the cry of 'heave' every man strained to lift his part of the bent the required distance and hold it till other men could thrust poles into it. There was a breathing space and then again all eyes on the leader: 'He-oh-heave!' and another yard was gained."

The raising described by Elijah Kellogg was
even more colorful. " 'You've got to lift now, I tell
you, for it's a master heavy frame,' said Uncle
Isaac. 'We'll make two lifts of it; take it breast
high, then take breath, and up with it. Are you
ready, men?'

" 'Ready,' was the reply.

" 'Well, say when you're mad.'

" 'Mad,' shouted Joe Griffin.

" 'Up with him, breast high.'

"Up went the great mass of timber, with a shout,
breast high, while the boys propped it with shores,
that they might take a breath.

" 'Be ready with your pike poles, boys; up
with him.'

"Placing their shoulders beneath the corner and
middle posts, and applying the pike poles as the
frame was elevated beyond reach of their hands,
it rose slowly, but with extreme difficulty for the
timber was of enormous size, and it was difficult
for men enough to get hold to lift to advantage.

" 'Lift,' shouted Uncle Isaac, 'till the sparks fly
out of your eyes; it must go up: if it comes back it
will kill the whole of us.'

"By dint of severe effort, it at last stood erect,
in which position it was secured by braces and
stay laths."

As Ralph Moody explained,

"Slowly, slowly, like the turning hand of a clock,
the great uprights rose, hinged on the wide
tenons at their bases. Men with heavy wooden
mauls hammered the timbers to bring the tenons
exactly in line with the sill mortises, and those
with poles jabbed their pikes into the uprights to
steady them. As the frame came straight up,
there was a screech of tight-binding dry wood,
the great tenons wedged down into their mortises, and the frame stood alone."

To John Burroughs, the commands of the master
carpenter were much like those of a captain to
his crew.

"The boss carpenter steadied and guided the
corner post and gave the word of command,
'Take holt, boys!' 'Now set her up!' 'He-o-he!'
(heave all heave), 'he-o-he!' at the top of his
voice, every man doing his best. Slowly the great
timbers go up; louder grows the word of command, till the bent is up. Then it is plumbed
and stay lathed, and another is put together and
raised in the same way, till they are all up."

Such memories were surely common to all who witnessed men righting a bent weighing several tons by dint of muscle and bravado. Kellogg reinforced this view:

"It must be remembered that the barn was to be large, and timbers of buildings at that day were of enormous size; the sills . . . were ten by twelve inches, and the plates, beams, and girths [girts] in proportion; besides, they did not make use of the mechanical appliances of the present day; but up it went, . . . by sheer muscular strength and activity. To be smart on a frame was considered a great accomplishment."

When the last of the parallel bents, connected only by slender girts and lintels bridging the threshing bay, had been raised, it was time to lift and fit the continuous plates, which would connect them and bring the frame into true. As Burroughs recalled,

"Then [came] the putting on of the great plates, timbers that run lengthwise of the buildings and match the sills below."

No other timbers bore so many mortises, into which the tenons of the posts, braces, and in some cases studs were to be fitted. This required the efforts of a host of helpers, as Kellogg attested:

"The young men now sprang like squirrels upon the broadsides, that trembled in the air, in order to enter and fasten the ends of the braces and timbers, that were lifted up to them by those below. Men were clinging to all parts of the broadsides, already raised, with a broad axe in one hand and pins in the other, and walking along timbers that quivered on the pike poles of those beneath. . . . On every side resounded the cries 'Three with a witness,' 'Four with a witness,' 'Brace number four,' 'Brace number five,' 'Give beam,' 'Rack off,' 'Rack to.'"

With good fortune, all the bents and at least one connecting plate would be raised before the earned appetites of many laborers were rewarded by the noonday dinner. As Kellogg recounted, efforts toward this began weeks before:

"They built a rough shed and made board tables under it for those to eat from whom the house would not hold. . . . A few days beforehand, they procured the ox, drove him to the barn, and killed and dressed him."

As a boy, Ralph Moody helped prepare for a real New England repast.

"Bill and I set up plank tables and benches and the women brought pots of beans, brown bread, big roasts of veal and pork, and a dozen pies and pitchers of cider. When Millie called, 'Victuals is ready,' there were thirty-eight hungry men washed up and ready to eat. Everyone was laughing and joking, and Millie and Annie ran back and forth between the table and the kitchen, bringing more pitchers of cider, tea, hot johnny-cake, and more pie."

"Then [came] the putting up of the rafters," as John Burroughs explained. Roof structures varied according to region and time period. In the mid-Atlantic states, the South, and the West, convention dictated a series of paired common rafters in the East Anglian style, stretching from plate to peak and often supported midway by full-length purlins parallel to the plates and of similar dimensions. In some New England barn roof frames, however, huge principal rafters rose above each bent to support a series of shorter purlins, which in turn bore secondary rafters, or, as in the Fenno barn, roof boards. Rafter pairs were generally joined at the peak by lapped or fork-and-tongue joints secured with pegs. Occasionally, rafters in New England terminated at a ridgepole, which ran the length of the barn at the peak.

Paired rafters were pegged while they lay horizontally on scaffold boards, and then were raised together into position. This effort took place high above the floor, increasing the danger of a fall. Barn raisings were all too frequently accompanied by injury. The annals of Andover, New Hampshire, record such an incident in 1822:

"The weather was very unfavorable, being rainy in the most part of the day, but no person received any injury except Mr. Daniel Smith. A large joist fell from the beams, one end struck him on the head, knocked him down, split the jawbone in the center of his chin, and injured his shoulder."

Henry Wright, a native of Otsego County, New York, revealed a major contribution to the incidence of accidents:

"As the labor was gratuitous, the whiskey went round freely and many a serious injury was the result. But no matter. The whiskey must go round or the frame could not go up."

Recalled Elijah Kellogg of the topping off of one barn,

"The timbers of the roof were now raised, and a bottle of liquor being procured, Joe Griffin broke it upon the ridgepole, having first delivered himself of a poetic effusion, full of humor and sly hits, which was received with shouts, and pronounced first rate."

Henry Wright described the final ceremony of another raising:

"After the frame was up, the last timber placed, and the last peg driven, all took off and swung their hats and gave three cheers."

According to northern European tradition, the last set of rafters raised was often festooned with a pine bough, a bush, or a broom. As Ralph Moody noted, a story pole could also satisfy the rite:

"When the last nail was hammered and the last screw driven, Grandfather climbed to the peak of the roof and set the story pole for a flagstaff."

Humorous toasts often accompanied the completion of labors on the day of a raising. The topping of a frame for a doctor in New Hampshire was chronicled by John Eastman:

"At a raising in 1818, a bottle of rum was broken on the ridgepole, and, from the same elevation, the following lines were delivered:

'Here is a fine frame raised on Taunton Hill. The owner is rich and growing richer still; May health come upon us like showers of grace, And the owner get rich by the sweat of his face.'"

The raising day was rarely brought to a close by toasts at the peak. One popular sport among the hearty participants was wrestling. Francis Underwood recalled a form of the sport called "pull up" or "pull the stick":

"The two antagonists sat on the ground facing each other, their legs extended so that the soles of each were squarely against those of his adversary. A smooth round stick, some two or three feet in length, held transversely, was grasped by both, and at a word each endeavored to pull the other enough to lift him from the ground."

Though these contests no doubt continued until every raiser had found his match, the activities of the day were not limited to wrestling. As Anne Gertrude Sneller remembered,

"As soon as the last nail had been driven, there was a dance on the big barn floor. On that ninety-foot-long floor the dancers had room aplenty to bow, circle, gallop, and swing. The musicians, never more than three for such occasions, sat in the empty hayloft and played until two o'clock in the morning."

A Raising at Brier-Patch

THE SEVENTH OF OCTOBER, 1989, dawned crisp and bright. The great day had arrived. Even before the sun had burned off the dew, family, friends, and neighbors had begun to gather for a modern version of a centuries-old tradition — a barn raising.

Months of preparation preceded this day. The small forebay barn to be raised was first constructed before the middle of the nineteenth century by a man named Chamberline on a slope of his farm in Sand Brook, New Jersey. For a century it housed the crops and livestock of Chamberline and his descendants; then it was moved to a neighboring farm. This was accomplished by jacking up the barn and rolling it intact on greased logs across frozen fields. The new cinder-block foundation was poorly engineered, and its gradual failure, along with the prospect of other costly repairs, led the owners to seek someone to remove the precarious structure. Not eager to see the old barn destroyed, they were receptive when they received a proposal to dismantle the building and re-erect it on a farm about ten miles away. Beginning in late spring, the barn was carefully taken apart and trucked to the new site. A heavy rain caused the final collapse of the foundation a few days after the barn's removal.

Brier-Patch is the name of the small farm near Lambertville, New Jersey, where the Chamberline barn was reassembled. The barn joined a simple four-room house built around 1825, a wagon house and workshop, a woodshed, a privy, and a corncrib, loosely arranged along a sloping meadow. After an appropriate location was plotted, a substantial foundation for the barn was laid up in block and fieldstone. Next the timbers were repaired; in some cases replacement pieces were fashioned. The old sill and floor joist system was reassembled and a floor was laid. Framing members were inventoried and stacked in readiness around the site. The time had arrived for the raising.

Dismantling the old barn

opposite

Most modern barn raisings are accomplished with the help of a crane. At Brier-Patch the decision was made to forgo machinery in order to capture some of the spirit of an old-fashioned hand raising. The only mechanical aid was a gin pole, or rum pole, a time-honored tool that was fabricated for the job. This pole was a twenty-six-foot timber braced to a six-foot base and stabilized by three long ropes anchored to the ground.

A block and tackle was rigged on this mast to assist in the great lifts. Workers could move this device about the site and then tilt it by adjusting the ropes. Although not necessary for the raising, the gin pole was certainly helpful. The first job of the morning, once enough muscle had arrived, was to erect it in position for the first lift.

With the gin pole in place, the raisers began assembling the first bent on the barn floor. Many hands were required to align the tenons with their corresponding mortises before the joints were finally closed with the beetle. The old peg holes in each mortise and tenon were offset slightly, a process known as draw boring, so that hammering in the peg would pull the joint tight. Those who assembled the sturdy oak frame could not help but appreciate the craftsmen of an earlier generation, who had skillfully cut the joints so long ago.

The strategy for raising the bents combined hoisting by hand with lifting with the block and tackle. At the direction of the boss carpenter to "Heave ho!" some participants pulled the rope while others lifted together. The bent stirred, creaked, and rose slowly off the barn floor. Once the bent was overhead, the lifters paused and one by one grabbed pike poles that had been placed nearby. These poles of varying lengths, with an iron spike at one end, allowed the crew to push the bent all the way to a vertical position. At this point two long temporary braces were nailed into place to stabilize the assembly.

Where repairs or timber replacements had been required, adjustments and final fitting forced a maddening but inevitable delay. One post of the Chamberline barn had badly rotted because maintenance of the roof had been neglected, so a timber of similar dimensions was prepared as a replacement. Craftsmen had to use the mallet and the framing chisel to adjust the fit of the joints before peg holes could be bored and pegs pounded in.

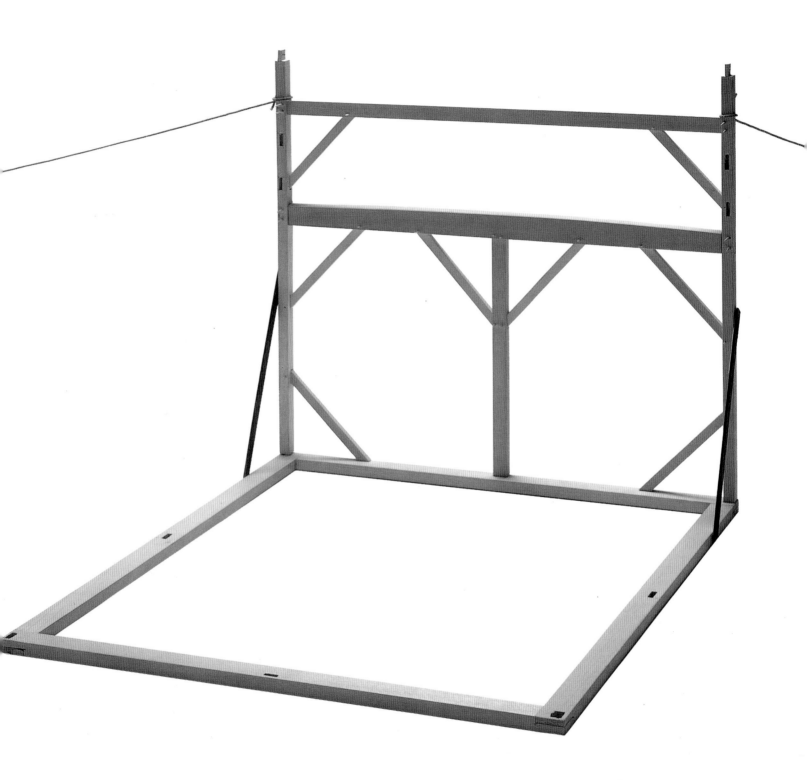

160

The barn raising took on a rhythm as periods of frenzy and excitement were interspersed with pauses for the relaxed preparation of the next stage. Dogs ran in the field, musicians played, and many participants sat and talked and watched until the next call to raise a bent.

After a short break, the timbers for the second bent were carried to the floor to be assembled. This section was heavier than the first, but the crew was now experienced and confident. Without incident they raised the second bent to a temporary position near the first, leaving room on the floor to assemble the third and last bent.

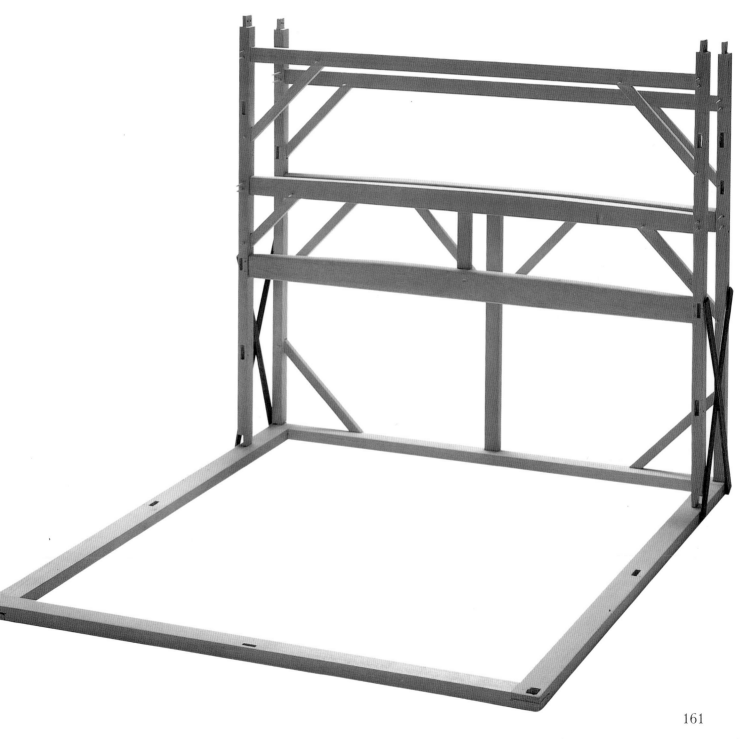

After a break for lunch, the crew transferred the
gin pole to the opposite end of the foundation
and rigged it to the third bent. On the boss carpenter's "Heave ho!" the last section was raised
into place.

With all three bents standing, two men walked the middle bent bit by bit into the center of the barn by prying with long iron bars. Next, after tying ropes to the tops of the posts, the crew tipped the bents out just far enough to insert the connecting girts and lintels. With these members in place, they were able to hammer home pegs to fasten the connections.

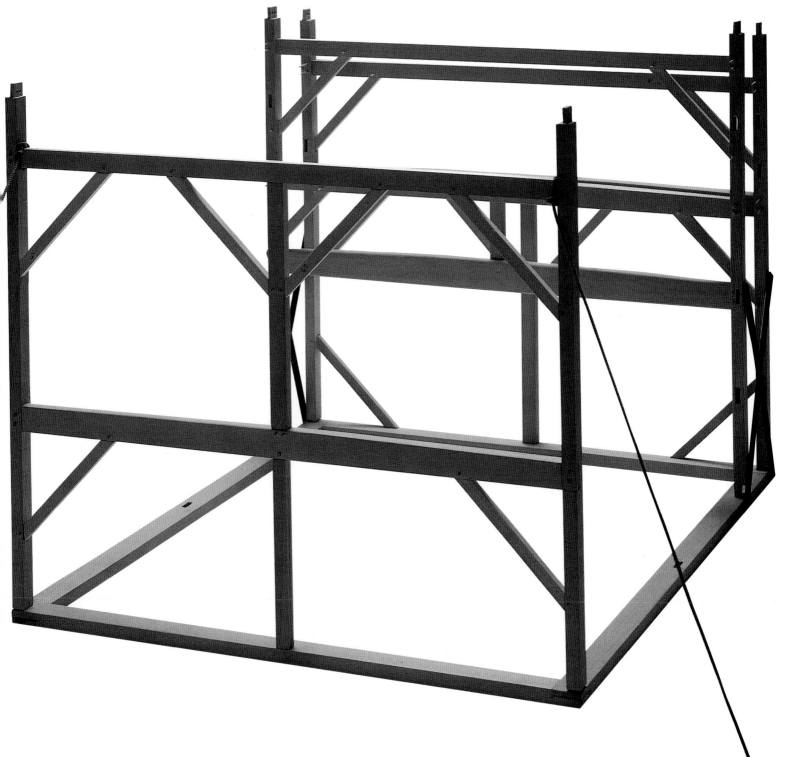

The next challenge was placing the rafter plates. These twenty-six-foot-long timbers run perpendicular to the bents and sit atop the posts on each side. Because sway braces need to be fitted at each post, many hands are required for assembly.

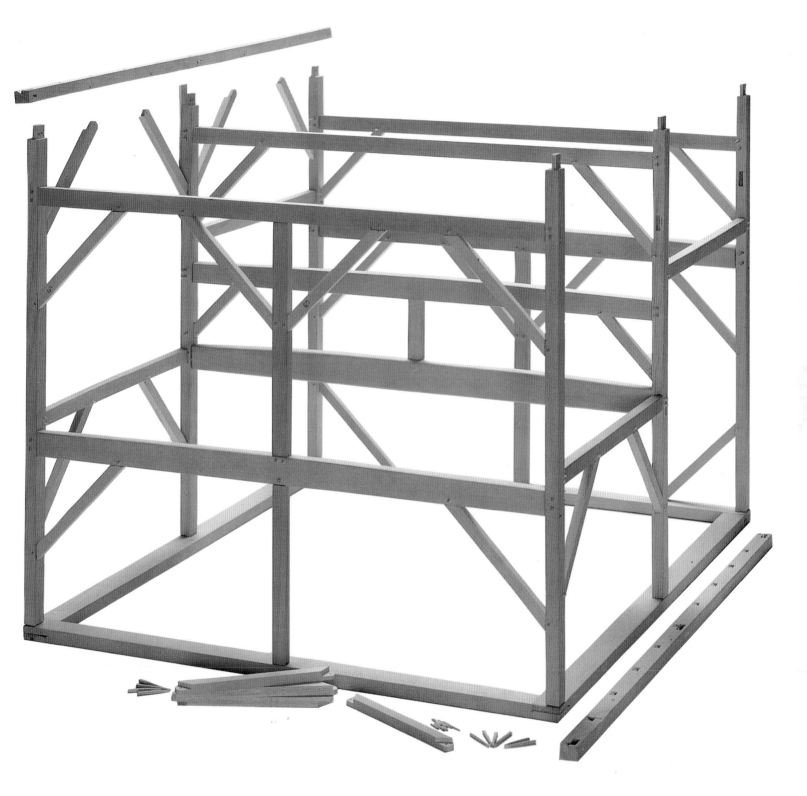

The crew placed scaffold boards between the
bents to provide perches before they passed up
the braces and tied them in place. The gin pole
was again moved and positioned to hoist the first
plate. In the last light of the day, the north plate
was wrestled into alignment one joint at a time
and tapped home with the beetle.

Tired but happy, the members of the crew climbed down and stepped back to admire what they had accomplished. Silhouetted against the sunset, the barn frame looked noble and grandly serene. There had been no injuries other than a few souvenir splinters, though there would be some satisfyingly sore muscles the next day. In keeping with barn-raising tradition, a festive dinner was served. As the autumn chill returned to the air, a bonfire made of scraps of wood that had accumulated on the site lit the faces of the newly initiated, latter-day barn raisers.

The following morning

The rafters start to go up.

The completed barn frame, before the addition

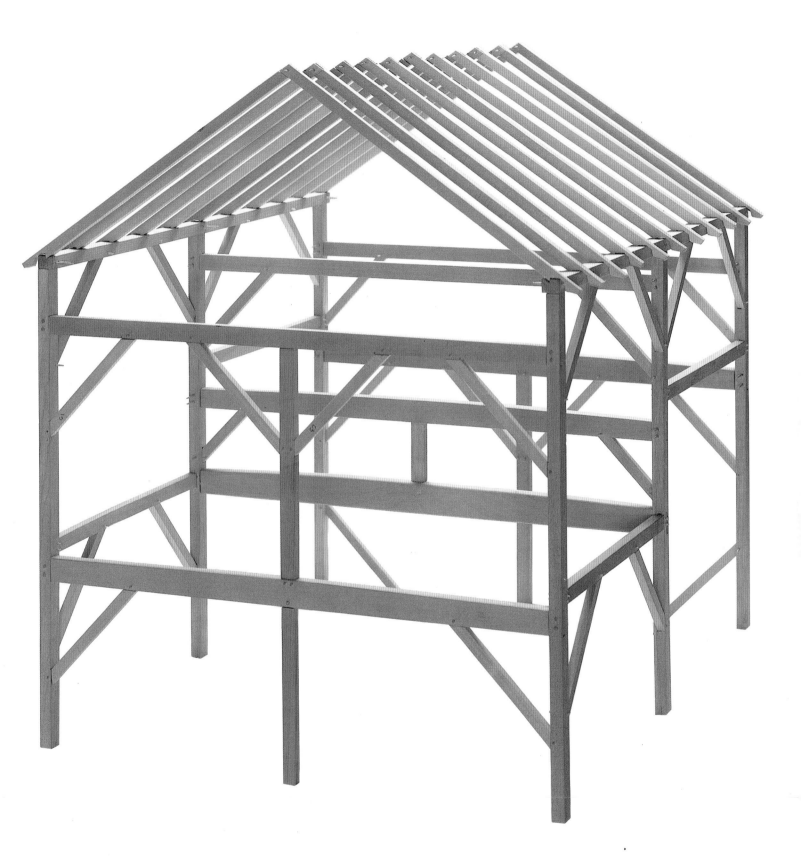

After a declared day of rest, work at the barn site resumed. In the following days a smaller crew raised the second plate, assembled the forebay, and placed the rafters. The tasks of roofing, siding, assembling and hanging doors, and inserting windows occupied the rest of the fall.

By the first snowfall, the Chamberline barn appeared comfortable in its new location. After a winter's weathering it assumed a timeless place in the landscape.

176

Living Barns

AT THE CLOSE of the twentieth century, barns have come full circle. The earliest tithe barns measured the collective cereal wealth of a wide domain. But yeoman farmers were quick to reduce the barn to its most essential uses, creating structures of three bays rather than ten or more. In Britain's highlands and on the Continent, barns were still more intimate, with family and stock often sheltering under one protective roof.

In America, relatively compact barns were sufficient to the needs of hundred-acre family homesteads, but as farm production expanded to feed the fast-growing urban populations, barn forms and functions changed accordingly. Wheat farming shifted to the Midwest; in the East, the primary crop became hay, which was needed to feed growing numbers of livestock. Barns of the late nineteenth century, though somewhat larger than in the past, were vastly more efficient because of new labor-saving devices and improved methods of cultivation and husbandry.

Today, the cost of fully mechanized farming has prompted yet another agricultural revolution. Though family farms still exist, they are increasingly anachronistic. Interstate highways have improved transportation, and refrigeration and chemical preservatives have extended the life of foods into a tasteless eternity. The truck farms serving a city today may be a continent away. And new barns, as always, reflect the character of contemporary agriculture. Efficiency is the essential aesthetic.

Constructed of factory-built trusses and sheathed in prepainted aluminum, today's barns provide uninterrupted spaces in which a forklift can stack more hay in an hour than a host of farmhands could stow in a week. Like the similarly capacious tithe barns of the Middle Ages, these giant warehouses shelter the wealth of thousands of acres.

Meanwhile, in the eastern states, expanding suburbs have made some of the richest land ever cultivated more valuable for housing than for harvests. The great barns of the past, forlorn and forsaken monuments to America's agrarian tradition, are gradually disappearing from the landscape. On today's farms, the old timber-frame barns are considered too small to be useful but too large to be feasibly maintained. Even now, when many of the best have already vanished, unrecorded by anything other than the capricious mind's eye, the value of these relics has not been widely recognized.

With the decline of the family farm along the burgeoning East Coast, America's most venerable barns have become its most vulnerable. Thousands are being destroyed, not only by the age-old scourge of fire but also by deterioration born of neglect, demolition in the wake of rapacious development, and wantonly unsympathetic conversion.

Without yearly attention to loose or fallen shingles, the deterioration of an old roof swiftly accelerates, so that rafters and other structural timbers are gradually exposed. Rot is the inevitable result. Too soon a heavy snow load or a windstorm will bring a once proud barn to its knees, as in the case of two forlorn relics in upstate New York.

"Regard must be had to the situation of a barn. It should be at a convenient distance from the dwelling house . . . but as near as may be without danger of fire."

— SILAS DEANE, 1797

"When I was a boy in Princeton we had two barn fires. The first was in 1913; I was then about seven. It was nighttime. My bedroom had a window looking toward the barn. I could see sparks coming over and burning little holes in the windowsill. I was trying to get dressed, but I was too scared. The fire company had a Buffalo engine and it pumped our well dry in about a minute. So the firemen got on the kitchen end of the house, which was closest to the barn, and they hung quilts over the end of the house, and what water they had they kept pouring on them. It blistered the paint off the house — oh, it was hot — but the house didn't catch fire. But the barn was gone.

"Well, my father built another barn, lovely, just like a house. And four years later, one night about seven o'clock, we were coming home from town, and my father looked up in the sky and it was red. 'Oh, my, that must be our barn!' And I remember him running all the way home. We had two engines there that time. But it all burned. And that was the end of it."

— WILLIAM HAHN, 1971

More appalling is the fate of the Cornell barn, built in Bucks County, Pennsylvania, in 1844 by the skilled and patient labor of many hands over many months. Well maintained throughout its agricultural life, it remained preserved by a sound roof until developers' equipment devoured it in a single day.

As part of a rich heritage to be preserved, each barn should be examined to determine which of a number of practical options may be appropriate. Many of these structures are simply unexceptional, and those who wish to preserve barns must be sure to direct their limited resources wisely. Many other surviving barns have already deteriorated too much to be saved. Nevertheless, it is important to record their features, including specific details, with photographs and carefully measured drawings. Although early barns fall into general classifications, no two are exactly the same, and it is only by creating a comprehensive record of the structures in a particular region that researchers can draw significant conclusions based on comparative data. Local historical associations should assign the same significance to farm buildings that they give to old houses and sponsor documentation efforts. Encouragement in the form of guidelines and grants from government agencies is also needed.

As family-based agriculture ebbs, many important barns remain in limbo for years while land speculators wait to harvest the greatest returns. Meanwhile, deterioration often provides an easy excuse for demolition. To stem this trend, it is crucial to maintain sound roofs on these barns. The minor annual investment of the time and materials needed to replace a few shingles or resecure a loosened sheet of corrugated tin preclude huge expenses in the future, and a small measure of maintenance can conserve a barn until a comprehensive restoration is possible.

How can barns be given a useful, adaptive new lease on the landscape? First, through farming. Despite the dominance of agribusiness in the production of grain and livestock, many family farms within easy reach of cities are finding profitable new markets for fresh produce and specialized crops such as berries and flowers.

Second, barns have always served as warehouses, and their vast spaces do not have to be restricted to sheltering animals or hay. The popularity of mini-storage facilities in the age of atticless condominiums suggests that barns could be profitably preserved as places to store cars, pleasure boats, snowmobiles, or other large or seasonal equipment.

Where farm roads have become highways, commercial use of a barn's grand, dramatic space offers a third interesting possibility for preservation, and there is no reason to limit such use to the familiar roadside antique shop. Banks, restaurants, offices, or churches that wish to root themselves in or near communities that value tradition would do well to consider sensitive conversion of local barns rather than contributing to the faceless superficiality of America's asphalt wasteland.

A fourth option is to convert small barns for domestic use, a move that was first tentatively undertaken early in this century by artists, actors, authors, and others who appreciated dramatic, romantic spaces. In recent years, the conversion of barns into houses has become increasingly popular among those seeking open, flexible contemporary space defined by massive timbers warmed by the patina of time. Collectors find in barns a satisfying backdrop for their treasures. For others, a smaller barn becomes the "great hall" of a house, central to family gathering, dining, and entertaining; bedrooms and bathrooms are relegated to wings or lean-tos. A barn house that incorporates appropriate materials and sensitive window design makes for an agreeable reuse of a traditional structure without diminishing its original rural character. These conversions work best without residential landscaping.

Outcroppings of stone throughout much of southeastern Pennsylvania provided an indigenous building material for early settlers and succeeding generations. Most of the stone was gathered as the fields were cleared. Enormous quoin stones, which had to be hauled up wooden scaffolding and set into place, were used to square the corners of barns and houses. Eventually, the massive walls of these structures demonstrated such an impressive feat of masonry that they became emblematic of the area.

Sad though it may be to see a fine Bucks County stone barn falling into ruin because of neglect, such quiet, gradual deterioration might seem a kinder fate than the rude transformation imposed on another small Pennsylvania barn. Here the unfortunate design of an awkward roof and fatuous fenestration have completely destroyed the graceful proportions of a barn conceived intuitively two centuries ago by a simple farmer.

Despite the fact that barns are no longer necessary in much of twentieth-century America, a few fortunate examples inspire dogged restoration. With patience and persistence, Elwood Long, of Oley, Pennsylvania, has rebuilt or repointed most of the stone walls of his barn, re-sided the forebay, and replaced the doors. When barns were the center of agricultural enterprise, safeguarding the farmers' crops and livestock, such chores were performed as required, mostly during the dormant winter months.

Exposed during restoration, the walls of Long's barn reveal the nature of early masonry. Square-faced stones, wedged with chinkers, were laid up in mud, then sealed or pointed with a final coat of sand-and-lime mortar. When the stones were as irregular as the ones in the Long barn, many builders chose to stucco over the whole job. When the mortar is intact, the walls remain impervious, but the cracking and decomposition of untended pointing lays bare the mud, which washes away, ruining an otherwise substantial structure.

No one knows when the first barn was adapted for residential use, but it was certainly long ago. In England many barns have been converted to houses, some successfully, others disastrously. In fact, the planning department of Essex has pointed out that "although residential conversions have resulted in many timber-frame barns being guaranteed an extended life, in most cases the conversion schemes have been poorly designed, and, despite considerable efforts by planning authorities, have resulted in schemes which have seriously damaged the nature of the buildings: the barn character has been seriously modified, and the results have been hybrid buildings of very limited visual appeal, frequently quite unrecognizable as barns." The department's guidelines for barn adaptation include suggestions for structural repairs, internal spaces, windows and doors, walls and roofs, and site considerations.

Since dormers rarely occur on barns, they should not be introduced in conversions. This tile roof, although expensive to install, creates a pleasing texture and color and will outlast most modern roof materials.

Large external masonry chimneys lend barns a residential character that it is best to avoid. A slender metal flue positioned unobtrusively is often a better solution. When possible, the roof should retain its original form and material.

The most sympathetic conversions are achieved by respecting the spaces and materials that give the barn its character. According to Gillian Darley in her book *The Farm,* "The quality of the conversion is usually the key to success, and many barns have been converted . . . without jarring the landscape or losing the major features of the original building. Unfortunately, the good examples are many times outnumbered by ill-considered conversions in which knickknackery drives out every worthwhile characteristic of the building. Some converted barns would have been better demolished."

No matter how radical the interior modifications, converted barns are most successful when the exterior presents its original face to the surrounding landscape. The Acres Farm in Bradford, Berkshire, has been altered for light manufacturing use. The thatch has been renewed and the farmyard setting has been carefully maintained.

In 1987 a program called Barn Again!, sponsored jointly by the National Trust for Historic Preservation and *Successful Farming* magazine, began offering awards for the rehabilitation of old American barns. More than five hundred farmers in thirty-four states submitted projects for consideration. One of the merit awards was received by John Desmond, of Charlton, New York, who converted his twentieth-century dairy barn in Saratoga County into a barn for thoroughbred horses. The concrete floor was jackhammered out and the cow stanchions were replaced by fifteen horse stalls. Above these, the soaring hayloft within the gambrel roof is filled every summer, then gradually emptied.

Contest winners spent an average of $11,000 on their projects, a figure considerably less than the cost of a new metal building. By promoting innovative ideas for refurbishing barns, the Barn Again! program has helped raise awareness of the value of old farm buildings.

Many old barns have been destroyed in the wake of development; others have succumbed to years of neglect. But a fortunate few are being well maintained by property owners who appreciate them and provide the annual upkeep required to preserve them. The barn complex with the wonderful twin silos is on an estate in New Jersey overlooking the Delaware River Valley.

below
The ramp that once provided access to the wagon doors of a barn outside Philadelphia was removed many years ago when a residence was incorporated into the lower level, where livestock had been housed. The hay level above now contains unheated storage space and a basketball court!

Whenever a historic building is moved from its original site, its significance is diminished. Though moving old barns is rightly discouraged by preservationists, relocation is sometimes the best solution when a structure is imminently threatened by development or neglect. Through the years many barns have been moved or raised or turned to suit farmers' needs. The traditional method is to jack up the whole frame and roll it on greased logs or on wheels. For longer moves, barns are usually disassembled piece by piece. This is a dirty and dangerous job, requiring patience and experience.

Historical documentation, including oral history, deeds, and other records, may help date the building. Proper site documentation is essential and calls for measured drawings as well as photographs. Coded tags, stamped or inscribed with permanent ink, that correspond to the drawings are then attached to individual timbers. When the tags are in place, workers can take down the frame, either entirely by hand or with the help of a truck crane. A large barn that has been disassembled can be transported to its new site on a single tractor trailer.

After the Stryker barn was slated for demolition to make way for corporate development in Skillman, New Jersey, it was carefully disassembled, repaired, and moved to the Beaverkill Valley in upstate New York, where it replaced a recently collapsed barn with the same ground dimensions. Care was taken to assure that its exterior reflected characteristics typical of the Catskill region, where cellar dairies are generally framed and sheathed rather than laid up in stone. A wide stone ramp from the original structure is connected to the central threshing floor by a wooden bridge.

A scale model of the Stryker barn was made when the structure was about to be moved. The large central wagon doorways punctuating each broadside define the barn as an example of the English style. Like most substantial timber frames, it displays a number of wind-braces to assure stability. Less common are the long braces in the rear wall, which carry much of the weight from the central posts to the end walls to lessen the load on the cantilevered forebay. The use of a cellar level for livestock is another example of cross-cultural exchange, in this case between English and German-Swiss traditions.

190

overleaf

The interior of the Stryker barn has been
restored to its appearance around 1820, when it
was built. The original flooring was preserved
and reused. New shiplap siding was applied to
the studding. The most exceptional and individual features of the frame are the slightly arched
swing beams, which span thirty feet and are
connected by long passing braces to the tops
of the flanking posts.

Only the basement level of the Stryker barn
has been converted into year-round living quarters. The upper floor is reserved for storage and
summer gatherings. When the sliding doors are
pushed aside, the original threshing bay provides a fine view and a welcome breeze of a
summer's evening.

Although this barn near Sheffield, Massachusetts, has been converted into a house, it remains in the same family that has farmed the land for generations. The barn setting is traditionally a work area, informal and without decorative planting. Those who convert barns should maintain that farm characteristic and avoid suburban residential shrubbery. A barn house requires no landscaping; surrounded by rolling hayfields and hedgerows, it is itself an unquestioned feature of the landscape.

The basic elements in the exterior treatment of the conversion at Sheffield are pleasingly straightforward, particularly when viewed from a distance. In approaching such conversions, architects do well to let the barn itself dictate the design.

overleaf

Because it once served as the center of agricultural industry, the barn lends itself to the frank display of necessary hand tools, be they hayforks and baling hooks or skillets and saucepans. Though a barn may be vast in volume, specialized areas of the house created within it can be comfortably intimate.

The least intrusive barn house designs retain the qualities of open space and honest materials. The ladders that once enabled farmhands to descend from the haymows are equally appreciated by young family members today.

overleaf

Most multi-use barns of early America included one or more lofts on either side of the central threshing floor. For this reason a series of levels in a converted barn appears natural, as long as the loft areas are not fully partitioned and the original threshing area remains open to the rafters. At Sheffield this principle has been followed to good effect.

Introducing so foreign a feature as a chimney into an old barn is a challenge that is rarely met with success. The design and execution of this example in the Sheffield barn is a noteworthy exception. The innate ponderousness of a twenty-foot shaft of stone has been muted by surprising deviations and cleverly angled courses of local stones.

In New England and New York State, many barns include a traditional porch, which protects the entry with a projecting gable on the building's broadside. Even with the addition of a starkly modern stair, the porch of the Pace barn continues to serve as the main portal.

overleaf
The great strength of the timber-framing tradition lies in the economy of members, each of which performs a very specific task in bearing weight, providing tension, or bracing for rigidity. Extraneous timbers are rare. Functionalism defines the aesthetic. Secondary features such as doors, windows, flooring, and sheathing are similarly straightforward and utilitarian.

In converting a barn, it is important to maintain this integrity. Newly constructed features should be honest but visually distinguished from the original structure. The temptation to use hewn beams where they never existed should be resisted, and members should be left in their original positions. The open mortises and empty peg holes seen in the Pace barn tie beams show the intended placement of interior posts, which were shifted a couple of feet in the conversion. Though this alteration is regrettable, the posts are *not* pegged in their new positions, which allows the careful observer to distinguish old from new. Similarly, the choice of plaster as the material for the new partition wall is not ideal, but it clearly defines the wall as a modern feature.

The Pace barn from Vermont assumes its new domestic role while retaining traditional materials such as seasoned siding and flooring, stone, and glass. The large triangular sheets of glass in the gable, while providing plenty of light, unfortunately diminish the character of the original barn. The overall effect, however, is clean and simple. Color, texture, light, and space are essential considerations in adaptive reuse.

overleaf

Occupying the space where a hayfork might have hung in years past, a ceiling fan serves a no less useful function. By gently circulating warm air that has risen to the peak, fans promote an even distribution of heat, keeping barn houses comfortable and economical despite their volume.

The bold inclined purlin struts and floor joists of a former loft give the Pace barn structural drama. Such framing features in this and many other converted barns offer a focus for innovative lighting.

The simple solutions that farmers and carpenters brought to the design of sturdy stairways in bank barns, wagon sheds, and the like might not include the sweep and drama on which many contemporary architects seem to insist, but their honesty and modesty are worth emulating.

Despite the fields that still gave it prominence in the landscape, the Weaversville barn in Northampton County, Pennsylvania, lay too close to a new interstate highway to escape the impact of development. After years of disuse, it proved a tempting target for unappreciative youths, who set it ablaze. Fortunately, the fire was extinguished before major damage was done, but the owners, sensing their liability, decided to remove the barn. Instead of being demolished, it was documented and eventually re-erected in Southampton, New York.

Although the oversize windows give a false impression of the barn's size and the diagonal braces decorating the sliding doors are mere parody, the exterior of the converted Weaversville barn displays several good design decisions. Sheathing in shingles is appropriate, given the barn's seaside location. The slender metal flues that service the furnace and fireplaces seem more like ventilators than chimneys. The lean-to extensions are natural additions, in this case housing the kitchen and bathrooms. Segregating these elements allows more open use of the barn itself.

overleaf

The breezes that once blew chaff from the threshing floor now cool the central living area of the Weaversville barn. Serving today principally as a summer weekend retreat from Manhattan, the barn is still protected by the great doors to the threshing bay, which can be closed for security or conservation of heat. The warmth of the original oak threshing floor and the focus point of the opposite opening easily draw the visitor into the barn house.

The fourteen-foot-wide threshing door opening has been divided into a multipaned transom and glazed sliding doors, which are frankly residential yet fully complementary. The braced frame and unprotected rafters of the trellised porch are an architectural allusion that somewhat diminishes the genuine framing of the barn.

opposite

The largely unbroken space of the Weaversville interior creates a modern "great hall." While its function is domestic, not agrarian, the basic sense of structure and volume has not been altered in conversion. Viewed from a billiards loft, the living and dining areas are defined not by walls but by the framing itself. A flag nailed up by the barn movers to celebrate the completed re-erection has been left as a testament to the structure's odyssey from Northampton, Pennsylvania, to Southampton, New York.

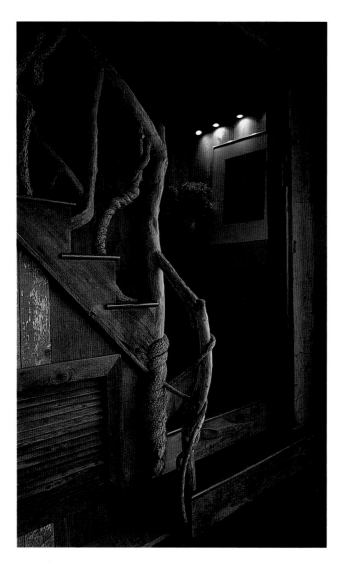

The staircase to the loft of the Weaversville barn manages to be both discreet and fanciful. Tucked into a corner beside the threshing floor, it does not intrude but assumes an identity that is reminiscent of Adirondack camps and reflects the owners' eclectic belongings.

More than a few collectors have found a barn house to be an attractive setting for their accumulated treasures. By nature, the structural simplicity and natural materials of a barn, when left largely undisturbed by a sympathetic architect, form a dramatic backdrop for folk art, found objects, Stickley furniture, and arts-and-crafts movement objects like those assembled in the Weaversville barn.

Although built in New Jersey, this example of Dutch-English hybrid framing now stands at Squibnocket on the south shore of Martha's Vineyard, Massachusetts. Just before its original site was to be paved for a parking lot, the barn was disassembled and moved. It happened to fit neatly on the granite foundation of a previous barn that had fallen into disrepair and collapsed. The interior framing remains true to its origins, but the outside reflects local characteristics such as the granite foundation and cedar shingles, which swiftly weathered in the salt air.

The sheer size of many American barns made them particularly vulnerable to the forces of nature, especially wind. To prevent the building from "going to rack and ruin" — an expression inspired by barns — timber framers employed a number of wind-braces in all directions. These not only help to keep the structure true but, especially when viewed in reverie from a rocking chair, provide a pleasantly rhythmic, sculptural beauty.

overleaf

Although insulated, the Wynkoop-DuBois barn is intended principally for seasonal use. Sleeping lofts, defined by waist-high walls, are the only additions to the interior. A low wing that includes living facilities, a kitchen, and baths satisfies the needs of the owner during winter visits from Manhattan. Although this barn is pleasantly sparsely furnished, barns can easily accommodate huge items such as armoires and billiard tables. At Squibnocket, before guest beds were added, a twenty-four-foot wooden sailboat dry-docked on the threshing floor provided bunks for four.

229

overleaf

The Squibnocket barn conversion is generally very successful. Much of this success can be attributed to the uninterrupted expanse of the barn interior. Many converted barns are recklessly partitioned, and the rhythm of the frame and the drama of the volume are lost. At Squibnocket the space is splendidly unspoiled.

Many barns include at least one practical innovative feature that is apparently peculiar to that building. The barn at Squibnocket preserves the tradition with a lofty gable window that has been hinged so it can be propped open from below.

opposite

The perspective through the threshing doors of the Wynkoop-DuBois barn once framed a view of New Jersey farmland, which later deteriorated into the clutter of a highway shopping center. Today, the length of the Vineyard's south shore stretches beyond the rainbow-roofed Cape that is the barn's companion on the landscape. The anchor beam in the foreground displays a string of mortise holes that once accommodated mow poles. Similar mortises on the outside face of the exterior anchor beams provide evidence that penthouse roofs once protected the thresholds. This feature, common to the earliest American Dutch barns, was employed well into the nineteenth century.

When a farm in Belvidere, New Jersey, was subdivided with typical disregard for existing structures, the property line was drawn directly through the old forebay barn. A newspaper advertisement for a buyer to remove the barn appeared at about the same time that a couple based in Manhattan were planning a country house in upstate New York. The husband, a well-known graphic designer, artist, and collector, envisioned a contemporary house with sunlit open spaces. The wife, a museum consultant, imagined a structure with historical character. The neat solution was the recycled, relocated Belvidere barn.

The wonderfully complex skeleton of the barn had been well protected by a slate roof. As the slates were cast off, workers were dwarfed by the structure's considerable size.

Once the massive haymow was cleared, the barn interior proved much larger than anticipated. The clean-out also revealed a legend proudly painted in foot-high letters on the breast board of the granary: "P.R. RUSH, BUILT 1862."

opposite

Planning a house without cutting or moving major timbers in the barn tests the skills of a designer. In the Belvidere barn, both intimate and grand rooms have been carved out to provide spaces for different moods and seasons. The two central threshing floor bays provide a wide-open gallery space. One end bay contains a kitchen and dining area, with family bedrooms above. The opposite end bay has been given over to a living room, surmounted by a studio and office space. Guest accommodations are in the basement.

The heavy oak timber frame is juxtaposed with delicate, high-tech steel bridges, which allow people to walk across the gallery between the separated quarters of the second and third stories. This feature does not pretend to be a part of the original frame. A bridge built with old beams would only have confused the order and intent of the barn design.

By the second half of the nineteenth century, hardware for sliding doors became readily available, and it did not take long for the American farmer to recognize the advantage of this new system. Sliding doors were adopted not only for large wagon openings but also for smaller doorways, both exterior and interior. In Theodore Roosevelt's barn at Sagamore Hill in Oyster Bay, New York, sliding doors on exposed tracks remind us of the utilitarian origins of the now meticulously detailed and decorated dwelling.

overleaf
One of the earliest barn conversions, Homer
Bigelow's studio, with hanging lamps fashioned
from milk churns

Although most barn house conversions have
been undertaken in recent years, it is interesting
to see how a Peterborough, New Hampshire, barn
was adapted into a studio for designer Homer
Bigelow at the beginning of the century. In those
pre-Bauhaus days, the influence of the arts-and-
crafts movement produced a pleasantly quaint
quality. The hanging lantern, for instance, was
made in the studio from a milk can.

Eventually the studio was winterized to become
a year-round residence. Today the barn is owned
by the fourth generation of Bigelow's family.

PRESERVATIONISTS agree that whenever possible, barns should remain on their original sites, to maintain the integrity of their orientation to the sun, the road, the house, and other farm buildings. These factors, in conjunction with cultural background, set the structure in its vernacular context. Unfortunately, the barns most desperately in need of preservation and the people who most want to preserve them are not always in the same place. Although removing a structure from its original site should be undertaken only as a last resort, it is better to document, disassemble, repair, and re-erect an exceptional barn in a new place than to demolish it. Ideally, a hospitable site will be found near the barn's original location, but circumstances sometimes dictate a move further afield.

EACH YEAR THOUSANDS OF BARNS DISAPPEAR. In those that remain for us to inspect and appreciate lie the vestigial remains of the virgin forests from which our country was carved. A barn's evenly hewn timbers and delicately fashioned mortise-and-tenon joints are testaments to the strength and skill of those who sought to tame a continent into cultivation. Traces of the day-to-day use of these structures are also present for us to discover and study.

Today, the land that these great barns were built to serve has been transformed beyond all telling, reflecting our complex and increasingly homogenous society. Unless we give sensitive attention to the immediate maintenance and eventual preservation of these monumental relics, we and the future generations who inherit the land will lose a link in the continuum of our culture.

A round barn in central Minnesota

Glossary

AISLED HALL An early framing system for halls, markets, and barns in which a central span is separated from side aisles by posts and braces.

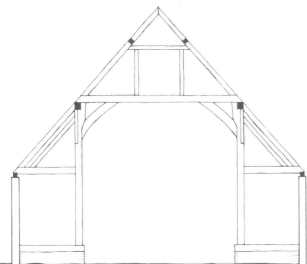

ANCHOR BEAM In Dutch barns, a massive horizontal member that ties together arcade posts to form a rigid H-shaped bent, which spans the threshing floor.

ARCADE POSTS Paired columns joined by one or more tie beams, which together form the nave of an aisled hall or Dutch barn.

BALLOON FRAME A type of timber framing introduced in the mid-nineteenth century, in which the studs are continuous from sill to plate.

BARGEBOARD or VERGEBOARD or RAKE BOARD The board on the outside of the gable wall that runs under the edge of the roof.

BASILICA PLAN A building plan in which a dominant nave is flanked by two or more side aisles. Dating back to Roman meeting halls, the form was adapted for early Christian churches. Later it was used in aisled barns in England and Dutch barns in the Netherlands and North America.

BENT The basic unit of assembly in a timber frame, in which vertical posts are joined with one or more tie beams and often stiffened with paired braces.

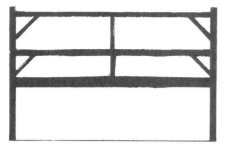

BRACE A diagonal timber, straight or curved, that is mortised into two timbers set at right angles to each other, to provide strength and rigidity.

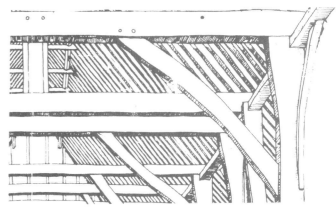

BREAST BOARDS Wide horizontal boards that form a wall alongside a threshing floor.

BYRE A cattle shed in Britain.

CANTILEVER BARN In the upland South, a barn form in which a second-floor loft projects beyond a log crib on the ground floor.

CLOSE STUDDING A timber-frame style in which tightly spaced vertical studs distribute weight along a wall rather than on major posts.

COLLAR TIE A horizontal timber that is framed between paired rafters to strengthen a roof.

COMMON or AMERICAN BOND A pattern of bricklaying in which a course of headers (bricks with the ends facing out) is set for every five or six courses of stretchers (bricks with the sides facing out).

CRIB A framework enclosure or stall.

CRUCK FRAMING A type of framing in which pairs of large curved timbers, or crucks, rise from the ground to the top of the roof, acting as both posts and principal rafters.

DOOR WITHIN A DOOR A small door set into a much larger wagon door for human use.

DOUBLE BARN A large barn with two threshing bays.

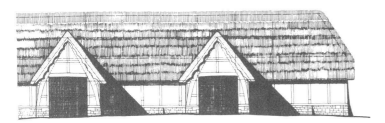

ENGLISH or **YANKEE BARN** A simple three-bay barn plan with a side entrance. Common in England and known elsewhere in Europe, this plan was used for most early American barns.

FACHWERK The exposed heavy timber framing of central Europe.

FLEMISH BOND A pattern of bricklaying in which headers alternate with stretchers in each course.

FOREBAY A projecting aisle on the downhill side of a Pennsylvania barn that provides shelter for livestock. Of German and Swiss origin, forebays typically face south.

FORK-AND-TONGUE JOINT A joint used to connect a pair of rafters at the ridge. The tenon (tongue) at the end of one rafter fits into an open mortise (fork) on the other.

GAMBREL ROOF A roof that has a lower, steeper slope and an upper, gentler one on each side.

GRANARY A storehouse for threshed grain.

GIN POLE A vertical pole anchored by cables, used with a block and tackle for hoisting and barn raising.

GIRT A horizontal beam between posts.

GRANGE BARN A huge warehouse for harvested grain, common to both monasteries and manors in the Middle Ages.

GUNSTOCK POST A post that flares near the top to bear both a plate and a tie beam; also known as a jowled post.

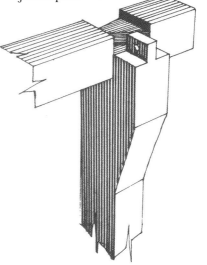

HALF-HIP ROOF See JERKINHEAD ROOF

HAY BARRACK In Germany and the Low Countries, a structure used for the seasonal storage of hay. Supported by diagonal pins set in tall corner posts, the roof could be moved up or down, depending on the size of the mow.

HEX SIGNS Colorful geometric decorations, typically in the form of a star, painted on many barns in areas of German settlement in southeastern Pennsylvania.

INFILL See NOGGING

JERKINHEAD ROOF An English roof form in which the upper portion of the gable slopes back to the ridge, forming a partial hip.

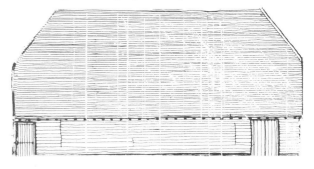

LONG HOUSE or LOS HOES A connected structure in France, Germany, or the Low Countries that contains living space for the farmer and his family at one end and space for livestock and crop storage at the other.

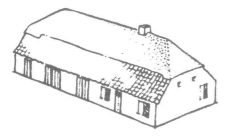

LOOPHOLE A vertical slot in a stone wall that provides air and light.

MARTIN HOLES Small openings cut into the weatherboards of the gables of New World Dutch barns, often in decorative patterns, to provide access for martins and other small birds.

MORTISE A slot cut into a timber to receive the tenon of another timber.

MOW POLES Saplings laid horizontally between tie beams to support the hay mow. Not part of the framed barn structure, mow poles were sometimes inserted into mortises at one end; the other end was left free so the poles could be moved.

NEW ENGLAND BARN Introduced in the nineteenth century, a popular barn plan in which the entrance is in the gable end.

NOGGING Any material, including stone, brick, or wattle and daub, used to fill spaces between studs.

OPEN LAP JOINT A timber-frame joint in which two pieces overlap but are not flush.

PADSTONE A large stone that supports a sill plate and rests immediately below a post to bear the building's weight. Padstones were used in place of a full foundation, particularly where stone was scarce.

PASSING BRACE A diagonal brace that joins three other members and is lapped where it intersects the middle timber.

PENNSYLVANIA BARN A two-story barn with a forebay, built into a slope. The dominant barn form in southeastern Pennsylvania, the Pennsylvania barn can also be found in the Midwest and Canada.

PENTHOUSE ROOF A shallow roof with a single slope, usually found just above the wagon doors on some English, Dutch, and German barns; also called a pent or pentice roof.

PLATE A horizontal timber connecting the tops of the outside posts of several bents and supporting the bases of the rafters.

PRINCIPAL RAFTERS Large, diagonal timbers at each bent that support the purlins, which in turn carry either secondary rafters or roof boards.

PORCH A roofed entrance to a barn or other structure.

PURLIN A horizontal timber running parallel to the ridge piece, supported by the principal rafters and supporting the common rafters.

PURLIN STRUT See QUEEN POST STRUT

QUEEN POST STRUT A pair of vertical or canted posts placed symmetrically on a tie beam and rising to the purlins or principal rafters.

RIDGE PIECE or RIDGEPOLE The horizontal timber at the top of the roof into which pairs of rafters are mortised.

SALTIRE BRACES In French timber framing, two long braces that are tenoned into the plates and girts and half-lapped where they pass, forming an X.

SILL PLATES Long horizontal timbers laid on the foundation to carry the floor joists and support the posts and studs.

SPLAYED SCARF JOINT A lap joint at the ends of two timbers with an angled cut to add strength to the connection.

SQUARE PANEL FRAMING A structural system in which a number of posts are connected by short girts at intervals of about four feet. Requiring relatively small timbers, this type is usually associated with German barns, though examples are also found in early English structures.

STUD An upright member of the framing of a wall.

SWEITZER BARN See PENNSYLVANIA BARN

SWING BEAM In some English barns, a beam that is large enough to span the width of the threshing floor without the support of a post in the middle.

TENON A projection at the end of a timber that fits into the mortise on another timber to form a secure joint when pegged.

THRESHOLD A board placed at the base of the doorjambs by the threshing floor to prevent the threshed grain from escaping.

TIE BEAM A horizontal member that connects two posts and provides structural support.

TITHE BARN A large warehouse built during the Middle Ages to house the tithe, a 10 percent levy on harvests charged by the church.

TRUNNEL or TREENAIL A wooden peg hammered through drilled holes to secure a mortise-and-tenon joint.

WALL PLATE See PLATE

WATTLE AND DAUB A type of nogging made of saplings woven between studs (wattle) and covered with mud and horsehair (daub).

A medieval cruck frame being raised
Drawing by F. W. B. Charles

Bibliography

Arthur, Eric, and Dudley Witney. *The Barn: A Vanishing Landmark in North America.* Toronto: M. F. Feheley, 1972.

Brunskill, R. W. *Illustrated Handbook of Vernacular Architecture.* London: Faber & Faber, 1971.

_____. *Traditional Farm Buildings of Great Britain.* London: Victor Gollancz, 1982.

_____. *Vernacular Architecture of the Lake Counties.* London: Faber & Faber, 1974.

Chappell, Edward A. "Germans and Swiss." In Dell Upton, ed., *America's Architectural Roots: Ethnic Groups that Built America.* Washington, D.C.: Preservation Press, 1986.

Clifton-Taylor, Alec. *The Pattern of English Building.* London: Faber & Faber, 1962.

Darley, Gillian. *Built in Britain: A View of Traditional Architecture.* London: Weidenfeld & Nicolson, 1983.

De Benaming van Houtverbindingen en Constructieve Houten Elementen bij Oude Boerderijen Een Poging tet Systematisering. Arnhem: Stichting Historisch Boerderij-Onderzoek, 1982.

Dilliard, Maud Esther. *Old Dutch Houses of Brooklyn.* New York: Richard R. Smith, 1945.

Ensminger, Robert F. "Comparative Study of Pennsylvania and Wisconsin Forebay Barns." *Pennsylvania Folklife* (Spring 1983): 98–114.

_____. *The Pennsylvania Barn: Its Origin, Evolution, and Distribution in North America.* Baltimore: Johns Hopkins University Press, 1992.

_____. "A Search for the Origin of the Pennsylvania Barn." *Pennsylvania Folklife* 30, 2 (Winter 1980–81): 50–71.

Fink, Daniel. *Barns of the Genesee Country, 1790–1915.* Geneseo, N.Y.: James Brunner, 1987.

Fitchen, John. *The New World Dutch Barn.* Syracuse, N.Y.: Syracuse University Press, 1968.

Glass, Joseph W. "Be Ye Separate, Saith the Lord: Old Order Amish in Lancaster County." In Roman A. Cybriwsky, ed., *The Philadelphia Region: Selected Essays and Field Trip Itineraries.* Washington, D.C.: Association of American Geographers, 1979.

_____. *The Pennsylvania Culture Region: A View from the Barn.* Ann Arbor, Mich.: U.M.I. Research Press, 1971.

Glassie, Henry. *Barn Building in Otsego County, N.Y.* Cooperstown: New York State Historical Association, 1974.

Hall, Donald. *String Too Short to Be Saved: Recollections of Summers on a New England Farm.* Boston: Nonpareil Press, 1960.

Hansen, Hans Jurgen, ed. *Architecture in Wood: A History of Wood Building and Its Techniques in Europe and North America.* New York: Viking, 1971.

Harvey, Nigel. *Old Farm Buildings.* Haverfordwest, England: C. I. Thomas & Sons, 1975.

Hubka, Thomas C. *Big House, Little House, Back House, Barn.* Hanover, N.H.: University Press of New England, 1984.

_____. "The Connected Farm Buildings of Northern New England: An Abstract." In Camille Wells, ed., *Perspectives in Vernacular Architecture,* vol. I. Columbia: University of Missouri Press, 1982.

_____. "The New England Farmhouse Ell: Fact and Symbol of Nineteenth-Century Farm Improvement." In Camille Wells, ed., *Perspectives in Vernacular Architecture,* vol. II. Columbia: University of Missouri Press, 1986.

Hughes, Graham. *Barns of Rural Britain.* London: Herbert Press, 1985.

The Jamesway: A Book Showing How to Build, Ventilate, and Equip a Practical Up to Date Barn. Fort Atkinson, Wis.: James Manufacturing Co., 1921.

Kalm, Peter. *Travels into North America.* Trans. John Reinhold Forster. Barre, Mass.: Imprint Society, 1972.

McManis, Douglas R. *Colonial New England: A Historical Geography.* New York: Oxford University Press, 1975.

Moffett, Marian, and Lawrence Wodehouse. *The Cantilever Barn in East Tennessee.* Knoxville: University of Tennessee School of Architecture, 1984.

Montell, William Lynwood, and Michael Lynn Morse. *Kentucky Folk Architecture.* Lexington: University Press of Kentucky, 1976.

Nicholson, John. *The Farmer's Assistant.* Albany, S.C.: Southwick, 1814.

Noble, John G. *Wood, Brick, and Stone: The North American Settlement Landscape.* Vol. II: *Barns and Farm Structures.* Amherst: University of Massachusetts Press, 1984.

Of Plates and Purlins: Grandpa Builds a Barn. Bethpage, N.Y.: Early Trades and Crafts Society and Friends of the Nassau County Museum, 1971.

Pruden, Theodore H. M. "The Dutch Barn in America: Survival of a Medieval Structural Frame." In Upton and Vlach, eds., *Common Places: Readings in American Vernacular Architecture.* Athens: University of Georgia Press, 1986.

Rideout, Orlando V. "The Chesapeake Farm Buildings Survey (Work in Progress)." In Camille Wells, ed., *Perspectives in Vernacular Architecture,* vol. I. Columbia: University of Missouri Press, 1982.

St. George, Robert Blair. "The Stanley-Lake Barn in Topsfield, Massachusetts: Some Comments on Agricultural Buildings in Early New England." In Camille Wells, ed., *Perspectives in Vernacular Architecture,* vol. I. Columbia: University of Missouri Press, 1982.

Shoemaker, Alfred L., ed. *The Pennsylvania Barn.* Kutztown: Pennsylvania Folklore Society, 1959.

Sloane, Eric. *An Age of Barns.* New York: Funk & Wagnalls, 1966.

————. *A Museum of Early American Tools.* New York: Wilfred Funk, 1964.

Soike, Lowell J. *Without Right Angles: The Round Barns of Iowa.* Des Moines: Iowa State Historical Department, 1983.

Stilgoe, John R. *Common Landscapes of America, 1580 to 1845.* New Haven: Yale University Press, 1982.

Upton, Dell, ed. *America's Architectural Roots: Ethnic Groups that Built America.* Washington, D.C.: Preservation Press, 1986.

————, and John Michael Vlach, eds. *Common Places: Readings in American Vernacular Architecture.* Athens: University of Georgia Press, 1986.

Vanderbilt, Gertrude Lefferts. *The Social History of Flatbush and Manners and Customs of the Dutch Settlers in Kings County.* New York: D. Anderson, 1882.

Vince, John. *Old Farms: An Illustrated Guide.* New York: Bramhall House, 1984.

Wacker, Peter O. *Land and People: A Cultural Geography of Preindustrial New Jersey, Origins and Settlement Patterns.* New Brunswick, N.J.: Rutgers University Press, 1975.

Yoder, Don, and Thomas E. Graves. *Hex Signs: Pennsylvania Dutch Barn Symbols and Their Meaning.* New York: Dutton, 1989.

Zielinski, John M. *Amish Barns Across America.* Iowa City, Iowa: Amish Heritage Publications, 1989.

Acknowledgments

We would like to thank the following for their help in the preparation of this book:

Elizabeth Ackerman, Richard Babcock, Ernest Born, James Boutwood, Walker Buckner, Joseph Butler, Don Carpentier, John T. Carr, F.W.B. Charles, Ivan and Jane Chermayeff, Evelyn D'Alesio, Gillian Darley, the Early Trades and Crafts Society, English Heritage, Robert F. Ensminger, Tom Farr, J. Barry Ferguson, Friends of the Nassau County Museum, Susan Fuller, the Galloway family, Adrian Gibson, J. W. Glass, Darrell Henning, Cecil Hewett, David Hill, Paul S. Hornblower, Curt and Judy Iden, Arthur I. Imperatore, International Association of Structural Movers, Garitt Kono, Lenny Larkin, Jo Carole and Ronald S. Lauder, Mark Mendel, Susan and Donald Newhouse, Rodney Pleasants, Peter A. Rafle, Jr., the Rural Development Commission, Robert St. George, Sheafe Satterthwaite, William Sladcik, Nancy Smith, Jack Sobon, the Timber Framers Guild, Sally Townsend, Jane Wade, Frank White, Alex and Carol Wojciechowicz, and the volunteer barn raisers.

Photographed by the bride's sister, a newly
married couple waltz on the old floor of the
family barn.

*The photographs are by Paul Rocheleau except for the
following:*

Tommy Candler, 184, 185

Gillian Darley (Edifice), 31, *top*

Alan Dench, 25

English Heritage, 18, 19

Robert F. Ensminger, 58, 74 *top*

Essex County Council, 16 *top*

Michael Freeman, 121, 122

Adrian Gibson, 30, 31 *bottom*

Joseph W. Glass, 95 *top*, 96 *bottom,* 107, 109 *top left and right,*
117 *top*, 123 *bottom*

Alexander Greenwood, 64, 65 *top*, 66, 72 *bottom*, 87, 93
bottom, 94 *top*, 95 *bottom*, 96 *top*, 104, 105, 106, 108 *top, bottom
and right*, 110, 111, 112, 113, 117 *bottom*, 124, 125 *top*, 176 *bottom
right*, 180 *bottom right*, 182, 188, 189, 190 *left*, 218 *top*,
226 *top*, 236

Fred Hoogervorst, 32–49, 62 *top*

Chuck Kidd (Old Sturbridge Village), 61 *bottom left,* 140–149

Malcolm S. Kirk, 62–63, 94 *bottom*

David Larkin, 12–24, 26, 28, 50–57, 61 *top left,*
176 *bottom left*

Norman McGrath, 237, 238–239

Tom Mason, 8

Joanna Eldredge Morrissey, 256

Rural Development Commission, 186

Sheafe Satterthwaite, 179

William S. Sladcik, 1, 6–7, 11, 120, 126–127, 128–129, 247,
248–249

Jonathan Wallen, 99

*We are most grateful to the following for permission to
reproduce from their drawings:*

Ernest Born, 26, 29

Frederick W. Charles, 18, 21, 138, 251 *top left,* 253 *bottom*

Cecil Hewett, 14, 15, 251 *top right,* 252 *right,* 253 *right*

Complex
Ridge
Post